no HR 4/21

12/15
8 —20

THE HAUNTING OF GREY HILLS
The Burning

JENNIFER SKOGEN

EPIC
Press

The Burning
The Haunting of Grey Hills: Book #1

Written by Jennifer Skogen

Copyright © 2016 by Abdo Consulting Group, Inc.

Published by EPIC Press™
PO Box 398166
Minneapolis, MN 55439

Cover design by Dorothy Toth
Images for cover art obtained from iStockPhoto.com
Edited by Melanie Austin

LIBRARY OF CONGRESS CATALOGING-IN-PUBLICATION DATA

Skogen, Jennifer.
The burning / Jennifer Skogen.
p. cm. — (The haunting of Grey Hills ; #1)
ISBN 978-1-68076-029-3 (hardcover)
1. Haunted houses—Fiction. 2. High schools—Fiction. 3. Schools—Fiction.
4. Haunted places—Fiction. 5. Young adult fiction. I. Title.
[Fic]—dc23
2015932717

EPICPRESS.COM

For Mom: my first reader, best critic, and biggest fan

Chapter One

Of course Macy knew the story of the school fire. Everyone in Grey Hills knew about the tragedy, but few could remember the names. The families of the dead children had mostly moved away right after it happened, and fifty years was long enough to turn unimaginable loss into trivia for out-of-town guests. Grey Hills had built a new school about a hundred feet from the old one and let a forest of alders and blackberry vines grow up around the charred bones of the original school. Some kids still told ghost stories about the burned students, but that was really just for Halloween. Adults frowned at these stories. *Think of the dead children,* they would say. *Think of the poor lost souls.*

Macy Pierce wasn't thinking about the Fire on the first day of her junior year at Grey Hills High. As she waited for first-period English to start, she thought about how schools smell like hospitals but not as clean. Macy thought about the crisp lines of her new jeans and how her ponytail felt lumpy. She kept touching the top of her head, trying to smooth the bits of brown hair that stuck up.

A few kids were already in class, filling the desks from the back of the room to the front. Macy sat in the middle and watched the clock tick toward 7:45 am. It was too early to be awake and too hot for summer to be over. The air conditioning didn't seem to be working and sweat pooled at the backs of her knees and in the crooks of her elbows. She wanted to lay her cheek against the cool surface of her desk, but that might look weird. The last thing Macy wanted was to be *weird* on the first day of school. They were already talking about her, she knew, and giving her the same sympathetic looks you might give a hurt animal at the zoo. *Poor Macy*, they would say. *Lost her big brother . . .*

As she waited, two boys came into the classroom. One she knew—Jackson Cooper. He entered the room like a storm cloud. Jackson was basically one big scowl with an emo-haircut. Macy had told her friend Claire to slap her if she ever started to frown that much. Jackson almost stopped at Macy's desk. She didn't look at him, but she could feel him slow down like a moon about to swing back around in orbit. Though he didn't stop after all, just kept walking to the back of the class and sat down with a loud huff. It was always like that with Jackson, he had to take up more space in the world than everybody else. This had annoyed Macy when they were friends, but she kind of missed it now. She didn't look back.

The other boy, though. He was interesting. Claire, whose mom worked at the school, had called Macy last week to tell her that there would be some new kids at school. Not new kid, but *kids*. Plural. Then Claire's voice had gone all squealy and Macy had to hold the phone away from her ear so she might have missed some of the details, but this boy had to be one of them.

In a school as small as Grey Hills, every new kid was a kind of exotic creature. One of those spiny lionfish in a trout pond. The new boy slid into the room after Jackson and looked around like he wasn't sure he was in the right class. He had thick black hair that almost covered his ears and skin that was a little darker than Macy's. He smiled as he walked past Macy's desk, and she flushed. When he took the seat right behind her, she felt the air move against the back of her neck. Macy wanted to turn around and look at him, but she didn't.

Then she felt a tap on her shoulder. She turned in her chair and met his dark brown eyes. He had those huge lashes that were supposed to be on a girl's face according to all makeup commercials. "Hey, I'm Dominick Vega. Dom. Is this English?"

For a moment she thought he was asking her if he was speaking English. Like, he was an alien disguised as a hot guy. Then she got it. "Yeah. Mrs. Polly's A.P. English. She's great."

"Thanks. This place is a maze. I walked through the cafeteria three times before I found this room. I have no idea how Trev and Sam are managing." Dominick grinned, shaking his head at the exploits of two people Macy had never heard of before. The other new kids? If there were three new *guys*, Claire would be unbearable. Macy laughed and nodded along like she understood. Then she turned around and went back to staring at the clock. Because she was cool like that.

Tap, tap. Macy looked back over her shoulder,

hoping the position didn't give her a double chin. "Yeah?"

"You didn't tell me your name. If you don't tell me, I'll just have to keep thinking of you as that girl with the pretty hair."

Macy blushed and muttered, "Macy," then turned back around. She heard him laugh behind her. She tried to place his accent. It was slight, but she could tell right away that he hadn't grown up near Grey Hills.

Glancing at the still empty door, Macy quickly took out her phone. *Dibs.* She pressed send then waited, grinning. *You found one???? Hot???* Claire always responded in seconds. Macy pictured Claire hiding her phone under her desk, texting by feel, her eyes up front like a perfect little blonde student. Claire always looked pretty damn angelic.

Macy was about to text back when she had the sudden feeling of being outside of herself, watching some other Macy smile and text about boys. Hot tears squeezed her throat and she put her phone away. Every time she smiled or laughed, or even thought about normal things, like boys or clothes, it hurt.

And it didn't just hurt the way she always thought grief was supposed to feel. Macy didn't just miss her brother—though she did miss him. All the time. She missed him the way she imagined a bird would miss her wings or a star would miss the sky. It was an empty, aching pain, and she didn't even know who she was anymore, living in a world without him.

Sometimes Macy was so mad at Nick that it felt like something molten and hungry lived behind her eyes. Other times she felt guilty about really stupid things. Here she was, texting her best friend. Nick would never do that. He would never get a new phone or search the internet for dumb cat videos or watch those new *Star Wars* movies. And that made Macy mad all over again. And guilty for being mad. He wouldn't take her to any more movies, where he always bought her a small root beer and her own medium popcorn even though they could have shared a large. He would never roll his eyes at something their dad said about the news or help her pick out a birthday present for their mom.

Nick would never . . . anything. Never live, never breathe. Never exist again. And it was all his own fault.

When the teacher walked in, Macy was trying not to cry. She got out her notebook and pen and wrote the date in the top corner of the first page. She blinked down at the lined paper, breathing in deeply through her nose and out through her mouth just like the counselor at the hospital had showed her. When Macy felt a little more solid, and the *I'm about to lose it in front of my whole class* panic started to fade, she looked up. The teacher, who was taking a stack of papers and a thin book out of his worn briefcase, was not Mrs. Polly.

Her stomach dropped. Had she just spaced on what room she was in? Or maybe Mrs. Polly was sick and they had a sub. Macy turned to see if anyone else looked surprised. Jackson was chewing on his pencil like a rodent, his feet propped up on the empty chair in front of him. Most of the other kids were either talking or just staring off into space. Dominick raised his eyebrows at her. Macy shrugged and turned back around.

"Hello class. I'm Mr. Bishop," the teacher said. "And this is the first day of the rest of your life." Mr. Bishop had thinning brown hair and looked to be in his late forties. He wore a brown suit that must have been hot. His glasses were thick-rimmed and black, like the kind hipsters wore. Macy wondered if her classmates were going to make fun of him or applaud his style. She wrote down *first day of your life* because she wasn't sure what else to do.

Mr. Bishop held up a book. "William Blake. I trust you've all done your reading?" Macy glanced around at the class again. No one had a book out. No one even seemed to be paying much attention. Mr. Bishop opened his book. "Today we'll be discussing *The Tyger* along with some of Blake's other poems from the *Songs of Experience* and *Innocence* cycles. *The Tyger* is arguably his most famous work. Who would like to read it aloud?"

Macy ducked her head and slowly wrote down *The Tiger* and *famous*.

"All right, I see we lack inspiration today," Mr. Bishop said. "Well, we wouldn't want a halfhearted attempt at Blake. I'll read this one, though I expect volunteers for the next." He cleared his throat, made a sweeping gesture with his hand, then began:

"Tyger Tyger, burning bright,
In the forests of the night;
What immortal hand or eye,
Could frame thy fearful symmetry?"

Mr. Bishop's deep voice filled the room. He had adopted a British accent for the poem and sounded like someone performing Shakespeare. He paused. "Anyone notice the meter? The use of alliteration?

The divine imagery? There should be raised hands when I'm finished."

He continued:

"In what distant deeps or skies
Burnt the fire of thine eyes?
On what wings dare he aspire?
What the hand, dare seize the fire?"

When Mr. Bishop came to the word *fire*, Macy saw him flinch. He paused and wiped his hand across his brow—he was really sweating in that heavy suit. "Excuse me," he said, then repeated the last line. *"What the hand, dare seize the fire?"*

He spoke slower, the dramatic flair gone from his voice. Then he stopped again, this time dropping his book on the floor. He didn't look very good—his face was red and he was blinking a lot. She wondered if he was having a heart attack or something. Should she go see if he was okay? No one else stood up to help, and Macy wasn't sure what to do. She didn't want to embarrass herself, or the teacher, if nothing was wrong.

While she sat frozen, still deciding how to act, Mr. Bishop's legs burst into flames. It happened so fast that Macy didn't even know what she was seeing at first. The flames, as they snaked up from the teacher's leather shoes, were almost colorless under the florescent lights. They covered his legs, curled around his waist, and engulfed his whole form in translucent ribbons of fire. His suit began to burn away, revealing patches of red, cracking skin. Within the writhing column of flames—which rippled a faint orange, and then blue—Macy saw Mr. Bishop put his hands over his face. The backs of his hands started to blister and blacken. The air smelled like burnt hair. He was screaming.

It was his scream that brought Macy back to her body. She stood up, knocking over her desk. Her own scream caught at the base of her throat, and she couldn't breathe. *Water*, she thought. *Fire trucks.* She thought of birthday candles becoming puddles of colored wax. She thought of a picture she had seen in history last year, of a monk who set himself on fire. But before Macy could do anything useful, like grab the fire extinguisher that was bolted to the wall by the door, or call 911, the teacher vanished.

He didn't burn up—he simply disappeared. Everything was gone: the rushing sound of the flames, the horrible smell. His ragged screams were gone, too, though Macy could still hear his voice echoing in her ears like the ringing after a concert. Macy pointed to the empty space at the front of the room where he had just been burning. Her whole body was shaking.

"Where . . . ?" She swallowed, looking wildly around the room. "The teacher, where did he . . . ?"

In the back of the room, Jackson stood up too, dropping his chewed pencil. "Macy? Mace? You okay?"

The room was silent for a long moment. Macy could hear Jackson's pencil roll under a desk. Then someone laughed. It was a nervous laughter—the kind that might bubble up at a funeral. The kind that can't be helped. Soon half the class was laughing and the other half was whispering. Macy heard "nervous breakdown" and "batshit crazy." She heard her brother's name.

Tears filled Macy's eyes. She ran from the room, pushing past Mrs. Polly, who was walking through the door. Just before she ran, however, Macy had looked at Dominick. The new boy wasn't laughing or whispering like the others. His eyes were closed and he gripped the edge of his desk, like he was trying to hold himself in place. Like he might just float away if he let go.

Chapter Two

Macy pushed open the door to the girl's bathroom and locked herself in the nearest stall. It smelled sharply of disinfectant. Though the walls had been wiped clean of most of last year's writing, there were still a few words carved into the smooth surface. *GO FUCK YOURSELF* stood out in jagged letters on the back of the door, just below a smiley face.

Macy sat on the back of the toilet, with her feet on the seat. She held her hands out in front of her face. They were shaking, and blotchy, like the blood had been squeezed out of them. They looked like a stranger's hands. Macy remembered the teacher's hands covering his face and how the flames had rippled across them. But it wasn't real. It couldn't have been real. A man could not just burn up while a room full of students ignored it. That could not happen. Macy kept looking at her hands because when she closed her eyes she could see Mr. Bishop's, covered with charred blisters.

The bathroom door opened. Macy held her breath, clasping her shaking hands over her chest. She stared at the word *FUCK*, willing the person to leave. The *K* was too long and trailed off at the wrong angle—the slip of a pen or knife. The person paused outside Macy's stall. His shoes were familiar. She could also see a thin stripe of jeans and t-shirt through the crack in the door. Meaning he could probably see her, sitting like an idiot on a toilet. Damn it.

Knock, knock. "Macy?"

It was Jackson. Macy did *not* want to see Jackson right now. If she saw Jackson a hole would open in the center of her lungs and they would both fall in. "Mace? You can't hide in the bathroom. Only crazy people hide in bathrooms."

Macy took a line from the bathroom wall. "Go fuck yourself, Jackson."

A pause. "Well, I do have plenty of practice."

"Go away." Each word brought Macy closer to tears. Her throat ached and she clenched her hands tighter to her ribcage, like she was trying to hold something in.

"I can crawl under. I'm still—what did you used to call me? Skinnier than a mosquito's dick?"

Macy snorted, then let out a ragged sigh. What was she doing? She stepped down from the toilet and opened the door. As soon as she walked out of the stall, Jackson wrapped her in a hug. She stiffened and turned her face away from his chest. He *was* skinny. Macy could feel the outline of his ribs pressed against her, the bones of his arms on her back. Jackson was tall, too, with a large nose and a face full of angles. His mother used to say that he would grow into his face, though she didn't live to see it. In class earlier Macy had noticed how his face had fleshed out a little over the summer, with sun-freckles scattering the bridge of his nose and the top of his sharp cheekbones. She was starting to see the adult he would one day become and it left her with a sense of vertigo at how quickly the world was speeding forward.

Jackson set his chin on top of her head. "Macy. Are you okay? I wanted to come see you after . . . " He trailed off, not saying the words.

So Macy said them for him: "After Nick died? You wanted to see me then?" She pushed him away. "You're an asshole."

"You're mad." His voice was pleading, and he reached out his hand to touch her shoulder. "I was mad too, when my mom died."

She brushed him away, then folded her arms across her chest. "We're not part of some club now," she said. Macy had never really wanted to hurt Jackson before, but she did now. "You don't get to *understand* me just because your mom's dead."

Macy didn't meet Jackson's eyes, but looked over his shoulder to the row of mirrors above the sinks. Her face was washed-out and wild: red, puffy eyes, lips the color of sand. She closed her eyes, then looked down at the fraying cuffs of Jackson's jeans. His dirty shoes. Without his mom to make him go school shopping, he was still wearing his old scuffed Chucks.

Jackson's mother had died about eight months earlier. Lung cancer. It was too fast. Crazy fast. They didn't even know she was sick and then she had only a few weeks left. Weeks are nothing. Weeks are a puff of air. Sally Cooper was the first person Macy had really known who had died. Macy thought losing Jackson's mom was the worst thing that could happen—that grief could never feel more claustrophobic. Her death was something you had to wear all the time—a coat you couldn't take off. Macy felt it when she sat next to Jackson in class, grief radiating from his skin like a sunburn. She felt it when they went to Jackson's house

after school and his dad looked fragile somehow—
thinner, maybe. Even the house smelled different
without Sally baking cookies or buying the right
laundry detergent.

Back then, Macy had thought she understood
Jackson, and that they were grieving together. She
didn't realize that Jackson was in a whole different
country, experiencing a degree of pain she didn't
even know could exist at the time.

The three of them always used to hang out at
Jackson's house—Macy, Jackson, and Claire. One
of Claire's revolving boyfriends sometimes made a
fourth. But it was usually just the three of them,
and more specifically, it was Macy and Jackson,
and then Claire. She had joined them in seventh
grade, when her parents divorced and Claire's
mom moved to Grey Hills. Macy and Jackson—
they were eternal. They had been friends since
preschool, when Macy held Jackson's hand and
Jackson didn't push her down or spit in her hair.
He later *did* push her and spit in her hair, but by

then it was too late. They were already friends and Macy learned how to spit back.

Jackson's parents had a basement that had been converted into a game room, with a huge TV, an X-box, and a Wii. There was even a full-sized fridge in the basement that was kept stocked with Coke for Jackson, root beer for Macy, and sparkling water for Claire—who already had eleven cavities and would no longer touch sugary drinks. There was also usually a twenty-four pack of beer at the bottom for Jackson's dad, and he never seemed to notice if one or two cans went missing. Macy usually smuggled the empties out in her purse.

After Jackson's mom died, Claire stopped coming over as much. Jackson was too moody, too hard to be around. But Macy was determined that things would go on as before. She did homework at Jackson's kitchen table. She ignored the awkward silences when she knew Jackson was thinking about his mom. She ignored Jackson's scowls and the temper he didn't use to have.

One afternoon, right at the beginning of summer, Macy and Jackson were watching one of their favorite movies. Something they had already seen a million times, so they didn't really need their brains to watch it. As they sat slumped on the couch, passing a beer back and forth, it could have been any time, any season. The curtains were drawn against the sun, and the only light in the room came from the flickering TV. Jackson had cranked the AC so high that Macy had goose bumps on her bare arms.

It was beautiful outside: the harbor shining, and the trees still clinging to the new green of spring. The kind of day that people who grew up in the Pacific Northwest couldn't help but savor like a luxurious bath. Claire's dad was visiting, and had taken her and her sister sailing. Claire had just texted Macy a picture of herself in a purple life-jacket and oversized sunglasses. Her blond hair was pushed back with a headband and hung loose around her shoulders. *U should B here.* Macy didn't reply, but felt a tinge of guilt, like she was literally wasting the beautiful day—pouring her summer down the sink like a gallon of milk.

Macy didn't like the taste of beer, but she liked the ritual of it: popping the top, Jackson letting her have the first sip, holding the sweating can in both hands. She liked that it was part of her and Jackson's world.

When Claire first moved to town, Macy had been possessive about Jackson and acted like she had a crush on him. She and Claire giggled when he walked into a room and wrote emails about what he had said or didn't say that day. But it was all pretend. Macy didn't really want Jackson in that way. All she wanted that afternoon was to sit with her friend in the dark and wait for his grief to evaporate.

When Jackson suddenly lunged at her—so quickly that she dropped the half-empty beer can, spilling it all over the arm of the couch and the carpet—Macy was shocked. She cried out, but his mouth was already on hers, his body pressing her awkwardly into the couch cushions. Macy had been kissed a few times before. There were middle school pecks and one lingering kiss at a school dance with a date she didn't even like that much. But she was not prepared for Jackson's tongue against her teeth, his fingers trying to unbutton the top of her jeans.

At first, Macy was too surprised to move. One of Jackson's hands pushed against her collarbone, just below her neck. She could feel her heart pound against his fingers. She couldn't breathe.

Close to panic, she had pushed him off. He grabbed her wrist, hard, then let go, moving away to the far end of the couch. "Fuck, Jackson!" Macy tried to keep her voice quiet because Jackson's dad was upstairs. "What the hell?"

Jackson covered his face with his hands. He said something that Macy couldn't quite hear. She leaned closer. "What?" Even though she was freaked out—adrenalin vibrating through her skin, her neck hurting from Jackson climbing on top of her—she still felt like she needed to protect him.

From his grief, perhaps. From himself. She touched his hands. "It's okay. We're okay."

He dropped his hands and looked at her, looked past her. "Leave," he said, his voice low and harsh—like a stranger's voice. Like a slap. "Go!"

She left him in the glow of the TV, in the dark basement that smelled like beer. But she texted him later, telling him again that it was okay. *They* were okay. He didn't text back. Eventually Macy realized something: Jackson hadn't been kissing *her*. He wasn't pawing at *her* jeans. What Jackson was doing was trying to disappear.

All summer, he was gone. Didn't return her calls or texts. Wouldn't answer the door when she knocked. His dad said that he just needed some space, but what Macy heard was *Jackson hates you. Jackson isn't coming back.* Then when Macy's life fell apart, Jackson was still gone. She hated him for it. And they were officially not okay.

In the girls' bathroom, Macy faced Jackson. She felt like she was standing on one of those moving walkways in an airport. Even though she hadn't moved, the distance between her and her old best friend was growing wider and deeper with every second. She wanted it that way.

"I know how you feel." Jackson spoke slowly, like he was talking to a child. "I know the world is fucked. I know you hate everything." Then softer, "I know you hate me."

Macy shook her head, finally letting the tears spill down her face. "You don't know anything. Your mom didn't kill herself."

Jackson sucked in his breath. "Nick didn't . . . It was an accident. He didn't want to die."

"Doesn't matter." Macy shook her head again and again, like she was telling the world *no*. *No* to Nick's death. *No* to the dozen beers. *No* to who knows how many shots of tequila. *No* to her brother's car wrapped around a tree. *No* to his unrecognizable face, his missing arm. *No* to the week he spent on life support.

"Doesn't fucking matter," she said, and walked past Jackson.

"Wait."

Macy didn't turn around, but she hesitated, her hand on the bathroom door.

"In the classroom, what happened? You really freaked out. That wasn't just about Nick . . . "

"It was nothing." Macy didn't have a tissue, so she rubbed her nose with the back of her hand, then wiped the clear snot on her jeans.

"You looked like you saw something."

"Nothing," she repeated.

"It's just, I thought I saw—"

But Macy was already walking away, the heavy door closing over Jackson's words.

Chapter Three

Macy went to her other morning classes, sat in the back, and hardly listened to the teachers. She felt numb: like the movie of her life had paused when she ran out of first period and she was waiting for someone to hit play again.

When she got to the cafeteria for lunch, the noise and press of people made Macy's heart race. This was new. Crowds had never bothered her before, but since her brother's accident she hated being surrounded. There just wasn't enough air.

She scanned the crowd for Claire, but didn't see her. Jackson sat at an empty table, looking at his phone. He glanced up when she walked by, but didn't smile or say anything. His brow was furrowed, like he was asking her a question. She shook her head and kept walking. It was strange to think that he had no other friends. Take away Jackson, and Macy still had Claire and a few other girls she could sit next to in class, smile at in the hall, and dance with in those girls-only circles at prom. Remove Macy from Jackson's world, and he was alone. He didn't even try. He just sat by himself with his sad slice of cheese pizza and his bottle of Coke from the vending machine.

Macy was so busy not paying attention to Jackson that she didn't see the man in the gray coveralls until he brushed past her, knocking her shoulder as he went by. She bit her tongue. The taste of blood filled her mouth and she could smell something wafting off the man—motor oil or grease. It reminded her of the kerosene lamps that her mom used to light when the power went out. The man looked back at her, just for a moment. He was wearing dark welders' goggles and was holding something metallic in his hands. A big oil can? Air tank? She wasn't sure. Macy swallowed her bloody spit and kept walking.

A moment later she found Claire sitting alone at a table that was covered with backpacks and littered with a few flyers for the Lock-In on Friday.

"What . . . ?" Macy began, gesturing towards the backpacks.

Claire cut her off. "I found them!" Her smile was maniacal. "These are their bags. They're sitting with us!" Claire wore a short blue dress (no more than two inches above the knee, per school policy) and silver leggings. Her hair was pulled back in a tight bun like a ballerina's, and silver hoops jangled from her ears. Claire always said she had a fat face, but Macy thought she was beautiful. Her face was more heart-shaped than fat—like a blonde version of the girl in the old *Pride and Prejudice* miniseries. The one with Colin Firth.

"You found who?"

"Come on, Macy." Claire rolled her eyes, giving

her an *I can't believe I even have to explain this to you* look. "I texted you!"

Macy hadn't checked her phone since first period. "I give up."

"The new kids! They're in line right now, I'm watching their bags." The three backpacks started to resemble a kill that Claire had dragged off the Serengeti.

"They're sitting with us? Why?" Macy had been looking forward to lunch because Claire would do all the talking and Macy could eat her crappy peanut butter and jelly sandwich in peace. She knew Claire wouldn't ask her about her freakout in English or bring up her brother. Claire's conversations were a big bite of cotton candy—light, fluffy, nothing. Macy was grateful.

"Because I asked. And they said yes. You know, like people do?" Claire took out her Tupperware of salad, an even smaller Tupperware of balsamic vinaigrette dressing, and a plastic fork. She stabbed a cherry tomato. "You met one already, right?" She smirked. "Dibs?"

Macy blushed and took a large bite of sandwich so she didn't have to answer. That was, of course, the moment that Dominick and the two other new kids took their seats.

"Hey—Macy, right?" Dominick set his tray next to her. She nodded, her mouth too sticky to say anything. Now that she could actually see him without twisting her neck, he didn't look quite how she remembered. His nose was slightly crooked and he had a little scar on his chin. His eyes were just as dark, though, and she tried not to stare. Did she remember to blink? Was she blinking too much? She looked down at her sandwich.

She waited for him to ask her about English, and why she had run out of class like a crazy person. But he didn't. Instead, he motioned to the two strangers who sat across the table next to Claire. "Have you met Trev and Sam?"

She swallowed the bite of sandwich—her tongue stinging where she had bitten it earlier—then answered, "No, not yet. I'm Macy."

Trev had light brown hair—almost red—and it stuck up messily. He had probably styled it that way. His eyes were somehow the same color as his hair. A smile tugged at the corners of his mouth. "Sure. We've heard all about you."

Macy tried not to scowl. She tried so hard that she thought there might be a vein popping out on her forehead, just above her left eyebrow. There were so many things to choose from—had they heard all about her dead brother or all about the desk she knocked over like a freak?

Then Sam cut in, "Claire told us that you like movies." Sam, it turned out, was not another guy. Sam was a gorgeous *girl*, with long red hair and eyes the blue-green of a mountain lake. Claire must be so disappointed.

"Yeah. I mean, most people like movies."

"But you'd know the best place to go see a movie,

right? In town?" Sam's tray was heaping with two large slices of pizza, a mound of tater tots, three cookies, and a chocolate milk. Macy didn't even know they'd give you more than one cookie. She'd never asked.

"Well, there's really only one place—the Opal. It's an old theater down on Main. Kinda small, but really cool."

Claire nodded. "There's a film festival this week. You guys should go. The Opal has great popcorn."

Dominick looked at Macy. "You want to?"

"What?" Oh, great, Macy—great.

"We could go see a movie. If you want . . . " Before she could answer, he added, "All of us, I mean."

"I'm busy tonight," Macy said, picking apart the crust of her sandwich.

"What about tomorrow?" Claire said, kicking Macy under the table. "I'm having dinner with my dad—but Macy's free. And isn't there a movie you wanted to see, Mace?"

Macy tried to glare at Claire while still smiling at the others. She probably looked ill.

"Yeah . . . *The Gallery*. But it's in French. And black-and-white. Real . . . artsy."

"Sounds good," Sam said. "I speak a little French. *Voulez-vous coucher avec moi?*"

"Singing along to the *Moulin Rouge* soundtrack in the shower does not count as 'speaking a little French,'" Trev said. Sam stuck her tongue out at him and then took a big bite of pizza.

"Okay." Macy attempted a more successful smile. "I think it starts at eight—do you need directions?"

Trev was already typing something into his phone. "Google maps. Age of miracles."

Sam flicked Trev in the temple with one of her long fingers. "What he means to say is that we'll meet you there."

"Are you two a couple?" Macy asked Trev and Sam before she could stop her stupid mouth. She always did that when she was nervous—blurted out personal questions like she was a reporter or something. Jackson and Nick both told her that it was really annoying, but it was probably the reason she and Claire had become such good friends in the first place. Claire loved to talk about herself.

"Macy!" Claire groaned in exactly the same tone she used when her mom did something embarrassing, like leave the house in her bathrobe to get the mail. The other three laughed.

"She's my sister," Trev offered, still smiling. "We weren't properly introduced. Trevor and Samantha Moss, at your service."

"Like Kate Moss," Samantha said, grinning.

"But," Trev said. "The moment incest comes back into style—you're my first choice, sis."

Samantha wrinkled her nose like she had just stepped in dog shit.

"Hey," Trev put his hands up. "Don't blame me. The Romans did it first. Or was it the Greeks?"

"They're twins," Dominick said, as though

that explained something about the current conversation.

"Yeah," Trev said, "but I got all the dashing good looks." This earned a snort from Samantha. Sam? Macy wasn't sure what to call her.

"Wait," Claire said through a bite of salad, pointing her fork at Dominick. "How do you know them? Did you meet at some *so you've just moved to the most boring town in the world* convention before school started?"

"Yeah," Macy asked. "Why'd you guys move here?"

Just then a scream cut through the lunchroom chatter and for a moment everyone went silent. It came from the lunch line. Macy stood up, trying to see over the mob of students gathering at the source of the scream. She could just barely make out a girl holding her hands to her head. A thin wisp of smoke curled in the air above her. It was Trisha Williams, who had long blonde hair that hung down to her waist. Or, used to: a huge chunk of her hair was now smoldering around her ears. Trisha kept putting her hands to her head and making little sounds that were half-breath, half-scream.

"Shit," Macy blurted at the same time Trev said, "Holy fuck." Claire dropped her fork, her mouth hanging open.

"It was Ian," someone called out. Macy realized there was a boy beneath the mob of students. A few people were holding his arms, others had his legs.

The new vice principal, Mr. Fitch, pushed his way through the crowd. Mr. Fitch looked like an actor playing a washed-up football star. He had thinning blonde hair and a bit of a gut, but his shoulders were broad enough to still be intimidating. He lifted Ian off the ground by his shirt collar and dragged him swearing through the lunchroom. Macy saw Ian drop a lighter and kick it across the room.

Some girls helped Trisha, holding onto her arms as they walked her to the nurse's office. When she passed their table, Macy could see that the skin along Trisha's neck was red and blistered and the collar of her shirt was burned. Trisha took deep, shaky breaths and the tears on her face glistened beneath the cafeteria lights.

Macy and Trisha weren't really friends, but she had the sudden memory of playing at Trisha's house with some other girls when she was little. Maybe it was Trisha's birthday party. It was summer and they ran through the sprinklers for hours, slipping on wet grass and laughing. Macy clearly remembered the weight of her own wet hair hanging down her back, the squish of muddy dirt and grass between her toes.

As Trisha left the lunchroom, the stunned silence began to fill with whispers. The school now had something even bigger to talk about than Macy's dead brother or her freakout that morning. Macy's phone buzzed. She had a new text. Jackson: *What happened?* Jackson was on the other side of the room and probably hadn't been able to see Trisha's neck or Ian being dragged away. She considered writing back, but put her phone away instead. Her hands were shaking and she didn't feel like typing.

"Jesus," Sam spoke up. "That must hurt like a bitch."

"Did you see her neck?" Trev added. "Brutal. She'll probably have scars."

"I'd kill Ian if I was her," Claire said, "I'd just rip his face off. Fucking psycho."

Macy set down her sandwich. She had been holding it so tightly that her fingers had gouged the bread. Off to the side of the room, just beyond the crowd, Macy noticed that same construction worker with the goggles—the one who had made Macy bite her tongue. He was smiling.

"You know who that is, right?" Claire asked.

"The construction guy?" Macy responded.

"Who? No, Mr. Fitch." She paused, recovering her fork from where she dropped it on the table and wiped it off with a napkin. "He's Principal Grey's grandson." While everyone else in the lunchroom was still talking about Trisha's burned hair, Claire somehow was eating.

Macy took another look at the man in the goggles. Claire *had* seen him, right?

"Grey . . . like Grey Hills?" Dominick asked. The others gave Claire their full attention.

"You've heard about the Fire, right?"

They nodded.

"Well, Principal Grey died in that fire. He was trying to save one of the students—his nephew, I think—and the ceiling fell. They were both crushed."

"That sucks," Trev said, stealing one of his sister's tater tots before she could swat his hand away. Dom took one of her cookies.

"Knock it off." Sam moved her tray away from the two boys and put her arms protectively around it. "But I thought Grey Hills was named after the bluffs."

The high, crumbling bluffs that loomed above the harbor were one of Grey Hill's most photographed features. Quaint Victorian houses perched on the edge of the bluffs, resembling birds about to take flight. Postcards in the tourist shops along the water showed this view: bluffs on a sunny day with the white flags of sailboats in the distance. Macy often wondered how long before the pretty houses would just slip off into the water.

"No," Macy spoke up. "A lot of people think that. It's actually named after the Greys—one of the founding families." Macy only knew that because of the local history class they all had to take in middle school. She thought the phrase "founding families" might make her sound smart.

Claire nodded. "After the Fire a lot of the Greys moved away. But my mom told me that Mr. Fitch had an aunt or someone who just died and left him a house. So he's back."

"Spooky, right?" Trev's eyes were practically sparkling. "He works at the school and the first day, there's a fire. Coincidence?" He suddenly reminded Macy of a leprechaun, with his reddish hair and the way he kept rubbing his hands together like he was plotting something. She wondered if he even realized he was doing it.

Macy shook her head. She was getting a headache and her tongue was throbbing. "It was just a douchebag stoner with a lighter."

She glanced back at the weird construction worker, but he was gone.

Chapter Four

Colleen, the fifty-something receptionist at the Western Winds Retirement Plaza, looked up from her computer as Macy walked in the door. "Macy! Did you see the fire at school?"

Macy stopped and stared at Colleen. "The fire?" She pictured Mr. Bishop's legs burning. She still hadn't mentioned the teacher—her hallucination—to anyone.

Colleen pushed her reading glasses onto the top of her head. They always tangled in her hair, pulling strands out of her already messy bun. "I heard some girl's hair was on fire. Were you there?"

"Oh, yeah. It was pretty bad. I guess Ian Randall

was playing with his lighter in the lunch line, and it caught on Trisha William's hair."

Colleen shook her head. "Drugs."

Macy waited for her to continue, but Colleen put her reading glasses back on her nose, pulling more hair loose, and went back to typing.

Western Winds Retirement Plaza wasn't the only old folks home in Grey Hills (the quaintness of the town made it the final destination for many retirees), but it was the nicest. From the front steps there was a great view of the water, and on a rare clear day you could see the mountains rising up in the distance.

Grey Hills sometimes felt like the middle of nowhere, especially when you were a seventeen-year-old girl without a car. The closest mall was a forty-five minute drive away, and you sometimes had to wait a while for the movie you wanted to see to come to the Opal. Other times Grey Hills felt like the center of everything. To the north, across the Strait of Juan De Fuca, was Canada. To the east (a ferry ride across the Puget Sound) was Seattle and civilization. And to the West, after you drove for miles along the very top of the Olympic Peninsula, was the vast Pacific Ocean. A lot of people saved up their money for years to move here when they retired, buying those whimsical Victorian houses and growing their own organic kale in their backyards.

Macy and Claire both started volunteering at Western Winds at the same time, but Claire quit after the first day. Claire had just said, "Old people stress me out," and the matter was closed. But Macy kept going back, and not just because it would look good on a college application. She just felt like a better person when she was there. That sounded cheesy, but it was like she had no excuse not to be pleasant and smile. Gone was the sarcastic, moody Macy that she couldn't help being when she was around her family. She was replaced by a smiling, respectful teenage girl who could produce small talk for hours. The weather, books, movies—anything that was pleasant and easy.

Sure, some of the residents gave her the creeps, like the one old man with a glass eye who stared at her chest with his good one. But most of the people were really nice, like grandparents. Her own grandparents lived in Arizona and she hardly ever saw them. Sometimes at Christmas, but there was this holiday cruise they liked to take to the Caribbean so they often just sent a card with a fifty-dollar bill inside.

If Macy had to get old—something she couldn't quite imagine, even after volunteering at Western Winds for almost a year (two hours a day, two times a week)—she wouldn't mind living there. The food wasn't even that bad. There were always plates of cookies sitting out and free coffee. Macy emptied four creamers and three packets of sugar into a green Western Winds mug and filled it the rest of the way with weak coffee from the dispenser.

Her teeth ached when she took the first sip—just the way she liked it.

Macy had missed the last three weeks since Nick died. Putting on her green shirt with the little Western Winds sailboat logo felt good. Almost normal. She helped out in the dining room sometimes, taking residents' orders. Other days she tidied the activities room and, if there was nothing that needed to be done, she would play cards with Esther Mckenzie. Esther was almost ninety, had been married four times, and liked to tell Macy about the men she had dated when she was a nurse in the war. Macy still wasn't sure exactly which war, but Esther looked old enough to have seen them all. She always had on bright red lipstick and, even though she was in a wheelchair, wore high-heeled shoes. Esther's favorite game was Bullshit and she cheated regularly.

It was too early for dinner so Macy checked the board. Bingo had just ended, which meant Esther was probably still down in the activities room. Bingo was actually really fun. Macy found it strangely satisfying to stamp her own card with those big thick pens they handed out. Macy wanted to tell Esther about Trisha's burning hair. Then, if she could stand the teasing, she would tell the older lady about Dominick. Esther was always asking Macy about the boys in her life, and now she actually had a sort-of date with a tall, dark and mysterious stranger. Actually, Dominick wasn't that tall. Way shorter than Jackson, but most people were.

The activities room was really posh—with a flat screen TV and huge potted trees that made the place look like a resort. It always smelled like orange cleanser and coffee. Some of the residents were reading or watching the news. Esther was in the far corner, her wheelchair pushed up to a card table. Carla Devine (who, Macy imagined, had been a stripper when she was young, maybe with the nickname Cherry) was showing Esther pictures on an iPad. When Esther saw Macy, she gave her a surreptitious eye-roll. Macy smiled.

"Hi ladies," Macy grinned at the two women. "Isn't it a beautiful day?" The weather had actually turned out a bit drizzly, but Macy tried to be optimistic.

Esther picked up her cup of coffee—a red gash of lipstick on the rim. "Honey. We've missed you." She always spoke slowly, her voice a little shaky. "Welcome back."

Carla looked up from the iPad. "I was just showing Esther the new pictures my daughter brought me. Here's my new great-grandson." The woman held the device toward Macy. The head of a red-faced newborn took up most of the screen. Macy thought he looked like a mole.

"He's precious," she gushed.

"Yes, well," Carla smiled. "My daughter says he takes after my late husband." Macy had the uncomfortable image of Carla as "Cherry Devine," dancing on a pole for a red-faced mole-man.

"I'm sure he does. So adorable."

Macy took a seat and told them both the news

from school. Carla put her hand to her chest. "Oh dear. Her hair?"

Esther adjusted her glasses. "A fire at school?" Her glasses made her already large blue eyes gigantic. Macy sometimes wondered how many men had fallen in love with those blue eyes. She also wondered how many of those men Esther had slept with, but she tried to keep those thoughts abstract.

"Just a small fire—an accident. No one was really hurt." Macy thought about Trisha's neck. She didn't actually know how badly she was burned. It hadn't looked good.

Esther pointed to a woman reading a book one table over. "Honey, did you know that Lorna was in the Fire?" When talking about the school fire of 1966, you didn't need to specify. It was just the Fire, capital *F*. Macy shook her head, though, when she thought about it, she remembered hearing that Lorna Evans had been a teacher.

Macy had noticed Lorna's scars before, but hadn't thought about them. At some point you don't question the marks and scars on an elderly person's body. It seemed invasive, like asking to read a diary. Lorna's right arm was a mass of scar tissue, from the wrist to where her floral shirt sleeve reached her elbow. There was also some scaring up her neck, where the flames had probably licked the right side of her face. Macy hoped that Trisha's neck would heal better than Lorna's had.

Lorna turned toward them. Macy knew she had been caught staring at Lorna's scarred arm, so she said, "I love your bracelet," nodding at the white charm bracelet circling the old woman's wrist.

"Oh, this." Lorna smiled, touching the bracelet with her other hand. "A gift from my grandmother."

"It's lovely!" Macy said. And it really was—tiny, delicate figures carved from what looked like ivory. "Where did your grandmother get it?" Macy had learned early on that the residents loved to talk about their family history.

Lorna frowned momentarily and Macy hoped she hadn't unearthed a bad memory. Once Macy had asked a female resident about her beloved dog and the woman had started sobbing (the dog had been dead for twenty years—like in that old song, "Mr. Bojangles"). Macy always tried to keep conversations light and cheerful after that. She tried to be Claire.

Lorna's brow cleared. "My grandfather gave it to her. He was a whaler in Alaska—these are made from . . . whalebone."

"Wow!" Macy had a flash of a young man dressed in a fur-lined coat, driving a harpoon through a whale's thick skin. She pictured bloody water and the whale's death throes. She could only imagine it as a movie—the reality of it, with the smell of blood and blubber, was beyond her. "He must have led a fascinating life," she said. History was Macy's favorite subject. That was probably another reason why she loved coming to Western Winds. Just talking to some of the people there was better than watching documentaries or reading memoirs.

They had actually lived through history—had been a part of it.

"Yes. He was a special man." Lorna picked up her book and turned away. Macy wanted to keep talking, to ask her more about her grandfather and Alaska, but she didn't. Instead, she told Esther and Carla about her upcoming date, then spent the next hour losing at cards.

Chapter Five

Macy had been looking forward to the Junior/Senior Lock-In since she was freshman. Actually, since Nick was a freshman and came home talking about it. On the first Friday night of every school year, the high school was turned over to the oldest students—letting them eat pizza and candy, drink pop, and sleep in the lunchroom in sleeping bags. The tradition had been going on for as long as Macy could remember, over a decade at least. Every year the students were warned that they would ruin it for all future grades if they weren't

RESPONSIBLE and RESPECTFUL. Of course, the students weren't left entirely to their own devices. A few chaperones were chosen to check in on them every now and again from another wing of the school. But for the most part the students were rulers of the school and they looked forward to it for years.

When Nick was a junior, Macy had asked for every detail. He told her to fuck off and wait her turn, but he didn't mean it. What Macy really wanted to know was what the senior prank was, and, more specifically, how bad it was. It was supposed to be kept a secret from the younger classes, but rumors spread. That year she had heard that the seniors waited until everyone was asleep, and then started shooting everyone with paintballs. Like, in the face and everything. Macy heard that a girl almost lost an eye.

Nick had just shook his head and smiled. "It wasn't that bad."

"So it was paintball guns? Did they have

night-vision goggles? Did they chase you through the classrooms?"

"Do you really think the school would let the seniors bring guns to school? Even fake guns?" But that wasn't a *no*. And the chaperones let the seniors get away with murder during the Lock-In. Everyone knew that.

When Nick was a senior, and she was a sophomore, Macy gave him constant prank suggestions: You could dress up like zombies and have fake brains to eat. You could wake the juniors up in the middle of the night with water guns. You could steal their bags and put them in the swimming pool.

"You are terrible at this, Mace." Nick had laughed at all of her ideas. She never did learn exactly what Nick's class ended up doing, but she knew it involved a lot of shaving cream, because he came home from the store with the back of his car full of those aerosol cans.

Last year's juniors were now seniors, and they

had started a countdown to the Lock-In. They put up a huge sign that hung above the juniors' lockers. On Wednesday, it said *3 DAYS*.

"The seniors are too stupid to think of their own prank," Claire said, taking her Advanced Calc textbook out of her locker. Macy was glad that her first class was not math. She needed to be awake for a few more hours before the math part of her brain came to life.

"Yeah. I bet they'll just cover us in shaving cream like Nick's class."

"Is that what they did? Sorry, Mace, but that's pretty lame." Claire was one of the few people who would still talk about Nick like he was a normal person and not some perfect saint now that he was dead.

"I don't think that's all they did . . . I bet it was really freaky at the time. Maybe they brought in black lights that made everyone look like zombies." Macy wasn't quite over her zombie phase.

"Uhm . . . still pretty lame. When we're seniors

our prank is going to give the juniors PTSD, and they'll probably wet their beds all through college."

"That's our Claire, always aiming for the stars."

"Damn straight."

Macy and Claire headed in different directions for first period. As Macy walked down the hall, Mr. Fitch appeared beside her. "Miss Pierce?"

"Oh, hi, Mr. Fitch. I'm not late for class, am I?"

"No, no. I just wanted to have a quick chat with you. I've already told your teacher." Mr. Fitch was at least six foot three and towered over Macy. He was wearing a button-up shirt with the sleeves rolled up, exposing his blond, hairy forearms.

"Uhm, okay." She followed him to his office, watching his broad back as they walked. Macy wondered why the old vice principal, Mrs. Doherty, had resigned. She was a chubby, short woman who looked like an owl, with round wireframe glasses and gray hair. Some students called her Mrs. Doughy, but Macy never did. After Nick died, Mrs. Doherty had sent Macy's family a card with a picture of a sad puppy wearing a blue bow. Macy wasn't sure how the sad puppy was supposed to make her feel better about her dead brother, but she supposed it was the thought that counted.

Mr. Fitch's office smelled like incense, which surprised Macy. It was fairly unpleasant—a cloying, cinnamony kind of scent. She sneezed.

"Have a seat." Mr. Fitch motioned to the chair across from him. "First, I want to say how sorry I was to hear about your brother. I'm sure he was a wonderful young man—all of the teachers spoke highly of him."

"Thanks," Macy said. She never knew what to say when people told her they were sorry. *Thanks?* Was she *thankful* that Mr. Fitch had now made her think about her brother during a school day? Was she *thankful* that she might start crying in front of a man who was almost a complete stranger? She swallowed and looked around the room.

On the wall was a black-and-white picture of the old school. It was a candid shot—probably taken almost a century earlier—of a crowd of people around the large, brick building. The picture focused on a pair of school boys walking down the front stairs. They were smiling and wearing those shorts and tall socks that you see on kids in old-timey movies. So weird that the building was now just a pile of burned rubble.

"You know I lost someone myself when I was about your age," Mr. Fitch said.

"Your grandfather?" Macy asked, still looking at the photograph.

Mr. Fitch seemed startled. "My grandfather? Do you mean Principal Grey?"

She nodded.

"I suppose—though I wasn't talking about him. I wasn't even born yet when the Fire happened. I'm only forty-three," he chuckled.

"Oh." *Only?* Macy couldn't imagine being in her forties.

"No worries. I was actually talking about my

sister. She was hit by a car when she was six years old. Died instantly. I was sixteen."

"I'm sorry . . . "

"Thanks." He paused, looking Macy right in the eye. She didn't usually make eye contact with teachers or other authority figures, and it was a little unsettling, like maybe he could read her mind, and he would know that she had been trying to avoid looking directly at his receding hairline and wondering if his hairy arms meant that he was hairy everywhere else too (except the top of his head, obviously).

"After my sister died, I acted out—especially at school. I stopped doing my homework, skipped class, and lied to my teachers. I didn't know how to handle it until I started talking to someone."

Macy knew where this was going. Mr. Fitch was going to bring up her freak-out yesterday and recommend that she see the school counselor. Or maybe a real shrink? They all must think she was crazy. "I already saw a grief counselor," she said. "At the hospital."

"That's a good start. And you know that the school counselor is available whenever you want. If you need to take a break from class and drop by Ms. Reyes' office, by all means. The teachers all know this is a hard time for you. But that wasn't exactly what I meant. Do you have any close friends? Someone you can talk to?"

"Yeah. I have some great friends." Macy meant Claire, but then she remembered, suddenly, how in third grade—after she got her tonsils taken out—Jackson rode his bike over to her house with a pint of ice cream, which had melted all over the inside of his backpack, and how Macy couldn't even eat it because the doctors had told her parents that she couldn't have dairy for two weeks.

"If you ever feel . . . out of control . . . like yesterday, please know that there are a lot of people you can ask for help. And my door is always open." It was open right then—the school must have a rule about male employees and female students. But Mr. Fitch did have a nice smile, like he actually wanted to help.

"Thanks, Mr. Fitch. I'll keep that in mind."

"And Miss Pierce," he added as she was walking out the door. "Have fun at the Lock-In."

As Macy walked to first period, she lifted her arm to her nose to see if she still smelled like Mr. Fitch's incense. No, thank God. She took slow, careful footsteps across the linoleum floor. It was never good to show up late for class, and after yesterday people probably thought she had been committed to an asylum and was never coming back. The last thing she wanted was to walk in that door and face everyone's stares and whispers.

When she reached the door, Macy paused. She checked her phone—no new messages. She ran her fingers through her hair and reapplied her lip gloss. After retying her shoes and making sure her backpack was zipped—twice—she finally reached for the door. Before she opened it, there was a movement in the corner of her eye. Turning her head, Macy saw the man in the gray coveralls leaning against the wall about ten feet away, next to a fire alarm. He was still wearing those dark goggles and seemed to be watching her. That same smell filled the air—gasoline, kerosene, something flammable.

"Hello?" Macy said. She regretted it immediately: why was she talking to a random construction worker? And what the hell was he doing in those weird clothes? He looked like he belonged in one of those steampunk video games her brother used to play, not in a high school. The way the man was watching her felt too familiar, too intimate. Like he was wearing x-ray glasses and now he could see her blue-and-white polka dot underwear. She felt dirty.

"I have to go to class," she said, pushing open the door.

As she entered the room, she felt a sudden heat on her back and could smell something burning. But when she looked back, the hallway was empty.

As she took her seat, Macy brushed a hand across her back. The rivets on her jeans were hot to the touch.

Chapter Six

Dominick and his friends were late.

Macy waited outside the theater for a full twenty minutes, fiddling with her phone and trying to look like she wasn't in the process of being stood up. Evening had brought a chill to the air as the town tried to let go of summer. Macy didn't have a coat and the salty wind off the harbor made her shiver. It had been a clear day, but now clouds were beginning to gather. Macy hoped the others showed up before it started to rain. She also wished Claire was with her, then she'd at least have someone to talk to. Going to a movie by yourself just looked sad. Macy would have called Claire to complain, but she was still at dinner with her dad.

The woman inside the ticket booth kept giving her encouraging smiles. Macy would half-smile back, then return to checking Facebook. They hadn't taken down Nick's page yet and occasionally one of his friends would still post something on his wall and it would end up on Macy's news feed. The first time it happened Macy had turned off her screen and held her phone against her leg trying to make her hands stop shaking. But now she looked for those posts. She didn't usually read the actual messages, but just scrolled through until she found Nick's name and picture.

When there were only five minutes left before the movie started, Macy bought her ticket and went inside. She hated missing the previews.

"One for *The Gallery*." She slid a twenty under the glass window. "My friends are late."

"Of course," the woman replied, sliding her

change and the ticket back. Macy didn't think the woman believed her.

Stepping into the Opal was like going back in time. The carpeting was the rich red of a 1920s speakeasy and the concession counter was polished wood that belonged in an old saloon. The faded, ancient wallpaper was covered with movie posters, and not just new ones: old Hitchcock movies, westerns, and Marilyn Monroe's playful wink were hung alongside new blockbusters.

Her favorite was the poster for *The Silence of the Lambs*. She used to think the Death's-head moth covering Jodie Foster's mouth was the creepiest thing ever. That was before she and Jackson actually watched it and decided it wasn't really a horror movie, but a detective thriller. It was still super scary, especially when Hannibal wore that guy's face like a fucking Halloween mask, but where were the monsters? When she looked up at the poster, where it still hung above the fountain drinks, Macy wondered again what it would feel like: the flutter of wings against her lips.

She didn't buy a popcorn or root beer, but went right into the theater. It was almost empty. That was what Macy loved about film festivals—there were always a few movies that no one really wanted to see and then you could have the whole place to yourself. A black-and-white French movie about a girl working in an art gallery was apparently not the most popular film in Grey Hills. An older couple sat near the front and a few college-age guys sat in the back. The guys were probably taking a film class and got credit just for showing up. There was only one other person, a young woman sitting right in the middle of the seats.

That was where Macy liked to sit: exactly in the heart of the theater, where the screen was as huge as it could be without having to tilt your head up and the sound wrapped around you. Most people didn't notice, but if you sat too far back at the Opal, you could see light filtering in through the edge of the doorway. Nick never noticed, but Macy could feel the light in the corner of her vision and it drove her crazy.

Macy sat one row behind the woman, and one seat to the right. She tried not to be annoyed that the back of the woman's head almost blocked the bottom left corner of the screen. It didn't actually block it, but if Macy tilted her head even an inch to the side she could see the top of the woman's head. She put her phone on silent as soon as the previews started. The others were still not there. She felt stupid for not getting Dominick's number.

About fifteen minutes after the movie started, Macy was surprised to see Dominick walking down the aisle. She ducked a little lower in her seat as he searched for her in the dark. A normal person would have sat up and waved, but she liked watching him. With the light from the movie flickering across his face, he looked like a fake version of himself—another projection that might vanish when the lights came on.

It didn't take him long to find her. He kept his head low as he sidled up the row, as though he might be blocking someone's view in the nearly empty theater.

"Hey, sorry I'm late," Dominick said in a loud whisper. He was holding a large popcorn and the smell of salt and butter made Macy's stomach growl.

Macy didn't ask permission before sinking her hand into the bag. "You missed the beginning," she whispered back. She wanted to be cool and aloof about the whole "date" thing, but she couldn't help herself. She was grinning.

"That's okay," he said. "I'll figure it out." He positioned the popcorn so they could share, then leaned back in his chair and put his feet up on the seat in front of him. He stared at the screen as though already absorbed in the movie, only moving to shovel popcorn into his mouth.

"Dominick?"

"Yeah?" He didn't lift his eyes from the screen.

"Where are the others?"

"You can call me Dom, if you want. Dominick's so long. Everyone shortens it eventually."

"Okay," she said, waiting for him to answer her question, but he went back to watching the movie.

"Uhm, Dom? Trev and Sam?"

"Oh. They couldn't make it."

The woman in the seat ahead of Macy kept turning around and looking sternly at her and Dominick every time they spoke. Macy stopped talking and tried to concentrate on the movie.

Macy was a little disappointed that the others didn't show. They were the kind of people you couldn't help but want to impress. She wondered if they thought the movie sounded boring. It *was* kind of boring. So far the main character had just wandered around the art gallery, looking at the weird black-and-white paintings. They were some kind of abstract art, with triangles and splotches of what Macy assumed were colors, but since the movie was in black-and-white, she couldn't be sure. Maybe the paintings were actually black-and-white? Macy would kill herself if she had to work in an abstract art gallery. She liked paintings that actually looked like something. The movie was probably supposed to be symbolic, but she hadn't been paying much attention.

Dominick spoke through a mouth full of popcorn. "Is the girl dreaming? Where is she?"

The woman turned again, glaring. This time she actually put her finger to her lips and shushed them.

Sorry, Macy mouthed back, then answered Dom. "I don't know."

"Those paintings are creepy. Do you think she's going to fall into one, like that little girl in *The Witches*?"

"I love that movie!"

The woman turned again and Macy's face grew hot. "Dom, I think we're being too loud."

"No way. This place is empty." He munched loudly on popcorn and put his feet higher up on the seat. The seats were old and his squeaked every time he moved.

Using her softest whisper, Macy said, "We're bothering her."

"Who?" Dom looked around.

"Her." Macy pointed at the woman, who had put her hand to the side of her head and sighed loudly.

Dom's confused expression dissolved into a broad grin. "I knew it. Trev owes me fifty bucks."

Macy's heart dropped and her smile turned into a scowl. Trev fucking *paid* Dom to go to the movies with her? "You came here on a *bet*?" She grabbed her purse and stood up. "Enjoy your fucking movie."

The woman gave an exasperated *harumph*. She looked up at Macy, and in the dim light her face was pale. She was young, maybe early twenties, and her lashes were long and thick. Her eyebrows looked like they had been drawn on with permanent marker, and her lips were dark. "Please do be quiet," she said in an exaggerated whisper.

"Sorry!" Macy hissed just as Dom grabbed her wrist.

"Wait. Jeez, you're touchy. Just wait a sec."

"Let go," Macy growled. She felt raw and exposed, like a live wire.

"This isn't a dare. I mean, yeah, there was a bet involved, but—no. I just wanted to show you something." Dominick let go of her, but kept his hand raised like he was trying to calm a wild animal. He took a deep breath. "Just sit down, please. I'll explain."

The couple at the front of the theater were now looking their way, so Macy sat, feeling flushed and foolish. That seemed to be her constant state of being lately—mortification.

"What?" Macy crossed her arms and looked back at the screen. A man had entered the art gallery and the girl was showing him one of the ugly paintings. They were laughing about something, but Macy had missed the subtitles and couldn't understand any French. She wanted to know what was so fucking funny.

Dominick leaned closer and she stiffened. "There's no easy way to do this. I wish there was, but there isn't. It's like a Band-Aid, you just rip it off. Or something. That's what Trev said, but that's stupid, right? I mean, don't Band-Aids hurt more when you rip them off? Sorry, I'm talking too much. I just want you to know that you're going to be freaked out and confused at first, but it's okay. It'll get better—I promise."

Great. She was on a date with a crazy person. At least a theater was fairly public. If she screamed, someone would probably try to help.

"Okay, here goes. Look at the woman in front of us. Really look at her."

The woman turned back around. "Some of us are trying to watch the film." Her voice was jagged. While the woman was facing them, Macy looked at her—really looked, just like Dominick had asked.

And when she *really looked*, she could see the light from the movie filtering through the woman's face. It was almost imperceptible: the way the woman's skin caught the light. It reminded Macy of the paper lanterns that her parents hung in their backyard in the summer. The woman glowed and when Macy tilted her head to the side she could actually see the movie playing through her face.

Macy gasped, then shut her eyes, tight. She *was* going crazy.

"You see her. I know you see her. I guess I could've just told you at school—hey, person I just met, I think you might be seeing ghosts. But what would you have said?" Dominick's breath was warm against her ear. "I mean, the chances of you believing me would have been basically zero, right? Trev and Sam thought I should show you. Trev bet me fifty bucks that you wouldn't be able to see her, but I knew it."

He sounded so happy, like he had just found

a puppy. Not like he was in a fucking haunted theater.

Macy opened her eyes and looked at the woman. She had already turned back to the movie and was touching the side of her face again. What she was touching, Macy realized, was a bloody hole in her temple. Now that she saw it, Macy couldn't stop seeing all the other things that were wrong with the woman. A trickle of blood ran along her ear and down her jawline. Bits of something—bone maybe? brain?—were caught in her long, dark hair. Her pale, translucent fingers kept touching the wound, then pulling back. Again, and again.

Chapter Seven

"She's not a ghost?" Macy whispered. Her words came out as a question, but it wasn't. She was trying to tell Dominick—tell the world, or maybe herself—that this couldn't happen. When she said the word *ghost*, the woman turned and stared at Macy, her face stricken. Her dark, glowing eyes filled with tears.

"She doesn't seem to remember most of the time." Dom's voice was lower, more serious than she had heard it so far. "She'll forget. Her kind want to forget." In a few seconds the woman's eyes cleared and she turned back around. Her fingers grazed her temple again, then pulled away.

Macy stared at Dominick. His face was no longer cute or mysterious. He was just a stranger and she had never felt more alone. Dominick let the silence pool around both of them until Macy felt she would drown in it. Finally, she whispered, "She's dead?"

"Shhh. She can still hear you." As Dominick said those words, the woman looked back at Macy and then vanished. "I think you scared her."

"What?" Macy had scared *her*? She stood up and looked over the back of the seat where the woman had been sitting, but it was completely empty. She was gone? Macy remembered how the burning teacher had disappeared. But that had all been in her head . . . right? Was she hallucinating now? Was this some kind of fucking trick?

"I found her on my first day in town," Dominick continued. "Trev wanted to take care of her right away, but I've been saving her."

"Saving her? Is that supposed to mean something?" Macy shook her head. "You're doing this. You and Trev had some bet . . . " She remembered then how Dominick had looked in the classroom the day before. His closed eyes. "You did it in English, too, didn't you? You made me think I'd seen that teacher. What are you doing to me?" Her voice rose into a shrill yelp, but she couldn't help it. She had to get out of there. Macy half-ran down the row of chairs, then sprinted out the door, through the lobby, and into the dark. It had started to rain after all, and her bare arms were immediately slick from the fine mist.

Footsteps followed her, then yells. Macy pushed past people on the sidewalk and then crossed a street without even looking for traffic. A car honked, but she kept running. The theater was only a few blocks from the water. Soon she ran out of road and jogged down a short flight of moss-covered concrete steps onto the rocky beach. Even though she had only been running for a few minutes, she found herself gasping for breath. Her head didn't quite feel attached to her body. Macy never believed that girls fainted in real life like they did in the movies, but now there were splotches of light darting on the edge of her vision and she knew that if she didn't sit down *right now*, she would fall.

Firm hands grabbed her arms and helped her down onto a piece of driftwood.

"Got you." It was a girl's voice.

"Dom, you must have been shit in there. Utter shit. Scared the poor girl right out of the theater." A guy's voice. Macy looked up at the sky, squinting through the tiny raindrops. She could just make out the shape of the moon through the clouds. Macy breathed in the damp, salty air—breathed so deeply that it felt like her lungs would burst. Then she screamed.

"Stop it!" A slap knocked her head to the side. Macy took another deep, gasping breath, but this time let it out in a ragged sob. Samantha stood over her, hand raised.

"You need to get a grip, girl. Calm the fuck down."

"You didn't need to do that." Dominick stood beside Sam. The moon was behind his head and it was hard to see his face.

"The fuck I didn't. Someone's gonna hear her. Think she's being raped or something."

"She'll be quiet now. She'll listen. Right, Macy?" Dominick sat on the driftwood beside her, but she edged away from him.

"Dom, you've done enough. She doesn't want you here." Trev pulled Dominick off the log and pointed down the beach. "Time out."

"You can't just give me a time ou—"

"Time out. Now."

"You heard him." Sam, who was a half-head taller than Dominick, also pointed. "Go."

"Fuck!" Dom kicked at the gravelly sand, then stomped away.

Macy started laughing, then covered her mouth. She didn't know why she was laughing. Nothing was funny. Not one fucking thing. Either tears or the rain streamed down her face. But she couldn't stop laughing. *Only crazy people laugh like this*, she could practically hear Jackson saying.

Sam crouched next to her. "Sweetie. Are you ready to listen?" Macy didn't really answer, but kept smothering her laughs with both hands. Sam nodded to Trev, who took out his phone.

"Okay, three minutes," Trev said, starting a timer.

Sam and Trev sat on either side of her. After a minute of silence, Trev began to hum. Sam shook her head at him, so he stopped humming and started picking up rocks and flinging them into the water. The soft *splash, splash* was almost comforting and Macy was suddenly exhausted. Her eyes were heavy and she yawned. She didn't know when she had stopped laughing, but that giddiness had crumbled in the silence and she felt dried out and heavy, like the log they were sitting on.

After three minutes exactly, Sam stood up.

"Okay. That's done. Better?" In the dark, it was hard to see Sam's features or the bright color of her hair. She looked so tall, like a statue.

Macy nodded, though she didn't know what *better* could possibly mean in this situation. She wasn't laughing to herself. She wasn't sobbing. That was an improvement at least. In the distance she could see the dark shape of Dominick pacing back and forth on the beach.

Trev stepped forward. "There are three things you need to know, then you can ask questions. Any questions?"

"Trev," Sam said in a low warning voice.

"Sorry. Joke. Anyway, three things. Number one," He held up his pointer finger. "There are ghosts. Yeah . . . that's kind of a big one. Number two, not everyone can see ghosts . . . You, obviously, can. Number three," he tapped a third finger. "We get rid of ghosts."

"We're not Ghostbusters." Sam added, and this time Trev shushed her. "I'm just saying, we don't have a ghost-mobile or those ectoplasm things. This isn't like some movie."

"Not a movie, got it." Macy said, a bit surprised that her voice was steady. She didn't feel fucking steady.

Trev then made a sweeping gesture with both his hands, much like a ringmaster at a circus. "Any questions?" He should have been wearing a top hat and a shiny vest.

Macy snorted. "Are you serious?" The cool, familiar wind whipped her hair against her face. After growing up in Grey Hills, the dark, gravelly beaches had become the landscape of her life. Sitting beside the water, with the town at her back, her head cleared and she began to feel stronger. She stood up.

Trev made a slight movement toward her, but Sam once again shook her head at him. He stepped back. "Is that your first question?" He laughed once, almost a seal bark, then began to rub his hands together. "I'm rarely serious. But yes. Right now I am."

Macy started to walk down the beach, slowly shuffling one foot after the other through the rocks and sand. If she kept walking she would eventually reach a lighthouse that was perched way out on a spit of land. She could see the pulse of light every few seconds, like a star caught too close to Earth. Long before she got to the lighthouse, though, she would reach Dominick. She wanted to talk to him—to hear him explain it.

"Question," she called behind her, as Trev and Sam followed.

"Shoot," Trev answered. He trailed by only a few feet, but didn't try to walk beside her.

"Why?"

"Specificity is helpful."

"Why do you get rid of ghosts?"

Dominick was still about twenty feet away and seemed to be digging a hole in the sand with a stick. He probably heard them approaching, but didn't look up.

Sam answered this one. "Uhm . . . because they're ghosts? I mean, you've heard of a ghost, right?"

"Casper was a friendly ghost," Trev cut in. "So Macy might be a tad confused on the subject."

"Ghosts are bad? Dominick said the lady in the theater was harmless."

"Really? He said harmless? Dumbass."

"I never said harmless," Dom called out toward them. He flung his stick out into the waves. "When did I say that?"

Macy groaned in exasperation. "I don't know what you said. I don't carry around a fucking tape recorder."

"You could use your phone," Trev added. "As a recorder, I mean."

"Not helpful," Sam muttered.

Macy made a noise between a groan and a scoff. "Okay . . . whatever. This is all nonsense."

"No, you were asking great questions," Trev said. "Gold star. Keep going."

"Okay," Macy said. "If that woman in the movie was a ghost—and I'm not saying she was—then why is she dangerous? She was just watching a movie. And," Macy pointed to Dominick, "you left her there."

"Yeah, well," Dominick looked to Trev. "She *is* harmless."

"See," Macy said, feeling as though she had proved a point—she just didn't know what that point was yet.

"Dom," Sam began, but he interrupted her.

"What's she gonna to do? Steal popcorn? I'll take care of it later."

"Hey," Trev raised his voice. "Guys, let's stop confusing Macy."

"Yeah, because that is the confusing part," Macy said, mostly to herself. The whole night still felt unreal, like she was going to float away if she didn't keep looking down at her feet. She wondered if there had been LSD in the popcorn.

When she was just a few feet from Dominick, Macy stopped. She had some idea that she should grab his arm and shake him as though the truth would fall out of him like a piece of fruit from a tree. Instead, she folded her arms across her chest. Goose bumps rose on her skin and her teeth started to chatter. She was so cold.

"Here," Sam said, draping something over Macy's shoulders. "You're freezing." It was her coat. "I guess chivalry's dead—right, guys?" Sam said in a loud whisper that Trev and Dom were sure to hear.

"I'm fine," Macy said, but she put on Sam's coat anyway. It was thin, and the sleeves were way too long, but it was better than nothing in the light rain.

"Now am I supposed to give you my coat?" Trev asked Sam. "And then Dom can give me his, and then Macy can give hers to Dom, because feminism?"

"No," Sam said. It was so dark that it was hard to tell but Macy was pretty sure that Sam was smiling. "You're supposed to build us a fire."

Macy held her hands out in front of the small fire. She was pretty sure they were *not* supposed to light fires on the beach, and she kept expecting a cop to come by and scold them or write them a ticket. As the flame gnawed on the small, broken pieces of damp driftwood, Macy once again thought of the teacher. Dom had seen him. That's what he said in the theater. He saw Mr. Bishop burning too. "So, you hunt ghosts?" she asked them, more casually than she had expected.

Trev answered her. "Yes. Exactly. Sort of. We go where we think there might be ghosts."

"Then you . . . get rid of them?"

"Yep. Can't just leave them hanging around. They get into all kinds of mischief."

"Mischief? What does that mean?"

Sam rolled up her sleeve. In the flickering light of the fire, Macy could just make out a long, snaking scar up her arm. "This kind of mischief."

"A ghost did that?" Macy felt foolish actually saying the word *ghost*. Part of her still suspected that at any moment the three of them were going to start pointing and laughing at her. *Fooled you!*

"Ghosts. Two of them, in New Mexico. One held me down and the other tried to carve something into my arm."

"Showoff," Trev said, poking at the fire with a stick.

"They aren't all that bad," Dom added. Sam made a snorting sound.

Silence followed as everyone watched the fire and listened to the sound of the waves. Macy tried to think of another question to ask, but her questions were too big to put into words. She still didn't quite want to admit that she believed them—that she accepted that ghosts were real. Finally, she said, "How old are you? Are you really in high school?"

Dom answered, "Yeah. We're real, live high schoolers. We just move around a lot. The schools think we're army brats. I'm seventeen."

"A gentlemen never reveals his age," Trev said.

Sam pointed at Trev. "My brother and I just turned eighteen a few months ago. We're actually adults, if you can believe it." Trev stuck his tongue out at her.

"So, your parents are in the military? Do they fight ghosts too?"

"No . . . that's just what we tell the schools," Dom said. Sam gave Dom a stern look before he added, "Yeah . . . Parents aren't really . . . a factor in this."

"You have no parents? Where do you live?"

Trev laughed. "We tell you about ghosts and all you want to know about is if Mommy and Daddy tuck us in at night? Do you want to know my favorite color and if I like long walks on the beach, too?"

"Blue," Sam said, then shoved Trev's shoulder. "And for the record, he loves long walks on the beach."

"Okay." Macy picked up a smooth rock from the fire ring and passed it back and forth between her hands. "You three can see ghosts, but most people can't? Why not?"

Sam winked at Macy. "Well, you know why you can see ghosts, right?"

Macy shook her head. Because this was all a dream? And pretty soon flying monkeys were going to carry her off to the Wicked Witch's castle?

"It's just like with unicorns," Sam said. "Only virgins can see them."

Macy glanced at Dom, then looked away. She hoped it was too dark for them to see that her face was burning.

"Sam, grow up." Dominick tossed a twig into the fire.

"Sorr-ee! You all just looked so serious." Sam ran one hand through her long hair, then twisted it over her shoulder like a rope.

Dom broke another twig. "Well it *is* serious. This is a job. We're not here to goof off and play high school."

Trev just kept looking back and forth between them like he was watching a TV show. Macy sighed, loudly, but no one seemed to notice.

Sam gestured toward the fire. "Am I playing? Was I playing last month when that ghost tried to rip out your throat and I stopped him? Was I playing in Texas when you almost got us all killed because you didn't fucking prepare? Jesus Christ, Dom. You think you're the only one who takes this seriously."

Trev tried to say something, but Sam cut him off with a chop of her arm. "No. You don't get to take his side again. You know what I'm talking about."

Sam turned back to Dominick. "You're the one

who thinks this is a game. You want to save them."
She laughed, loud and sharp—just like her brother's laugh. "You probably thought you were saving her, too."

She looked at Macy. "I'm sorry. He never should've brought you into this. It was selfish." Sam punctuated the last word by standing up. Macy saw her light a cigarette as she walked away. It was only after Sam had disappeared from sight that Macy remembered she was still wearing Sam's coat.

"Fucking hell. Sorry about that," Trev said, poking at the fire with a longer stick. "My sister has a bit of a temper."

Dom was perfectly still. His hands were folded in his lap. "She doesn't just have a temper, Trev. She doesn't think—she just does whatever the hell she wants. She's going to get someone killed."

Macy was pretty sure that if she melted into the sand right then, neither Trev nor Dom would notice. "Guys?" she asked. They both turned to

Macy, their eyes widening slightly as though just realizing she was still there. "Look, I get that you have your little club, with all your secrets and inside jokes and stuff. And I don't care—I don't give a shit what you guys are fighting about unless you can tell me why I'm seeing motherfucking ghosts!" She tried to keep her voice down, but she shouldn't have bothered. There was no one else on the beach.

It was Dom who finally answered her. "You can see ghosts because your brother died and it fucked up your brain."

"Sorry," Trev said. He held up the burning stick and drew something in the air with the smoke.

Chapter Eight

The porch light was still on when Macy got home. Moths fluttered around her hair as she unlocked the door, and one followed her inside. She tried to catch it, reaching out her hand towards the gray wings, but missed. It floated away into the shadows. Her cat, Jasper, would probably eat it.

"Good movie?" Macy's dad sat at the kitchen table, phone in both hands. He looked up as she walked into the room.

"Yeah. But I don't think you'd like it." Macy was starving. She grabbed a slice of bread from the bag on the counter, wadded it up in her hand,

and shoved it in her mouth. She did this without thinking—a childhood habit that Nick used to tease her about.

"Hungry?" Her dad's gaze slid back to his phone. He was probably playing Angry Birds. He did that when he couldn't sleep.

"A bit."

"Your mom made lasagna. There's some in the fridge."

"Kay," she said, but she just reached for a second slice of bread. And with that, Macy ran out of things to say.

For that first week after Nick's accident, when there was still hope, Macy had never felt closer to her dad. They suddenly had a shared language. *How was Nick doing? Had he moved his hand? Did he blink? Could he hear them?* They talked about the nurses (one was probably a man, but they weren't sure) and what hospital food was edible (the fries and ice cream, but not the fish). While her mother stared at her hands, Macy and her father had dissected the accident itself, as though they were discussing a great battle from history. Her father kept saying how it could have been worse—had Nick veered three more inches to the right, a branch might have gone through his trachea. If Nick had been going a little faster, the engine might have come through the dashboard and crushed him. If he hadn't been wearing his seatbelt, he might have gone through the windshield himself. It was as though they could keep him alive by speaking aloud all of the ways he didn't die.

They didn't talk about the alcohol or his missing arm. They didn't talk about how he might never see again. When her mom brought up plastic surgery, Macy felt her tongue stick to the roof of her mouth like glue. She didn't want to think about what would come after: how her brother would not be her brother anymore, but her brother who drank too much and crashed his car. The brother who had ruined his life.

After Nick died, it was like she and her dad were

refugees from another country—one they never wanted to talk about again.

"Going to bed?" her dad asked, his eyes back on his phone.

"Yeah."

"Night, sweetheart."

"Night."

Macy had to walk past Nick's closed door to reach her room. At first it had seemed like he might still be there in his room. Not anymore. It had been three weeks since he died, and now it felt like a painted door—a scene from that roadrunner cartoon. The roadrunner can walk through the door in the side of a cliff, but when the coyote tries it, it's no longer a real door—just a painting of a door. Macy hated being the fucking coyote.

It wasn't really that late. Maybe nine-thirty. She picked up her phone and almost pressed Jackson's number before she realized what her hands were doing. Everything Dom, Trev, and Sam had told her filled her head like another cartoon character, the Tasmanian Devil, with the information spinning and chewing the inside of her brain.

After Sam had stormed off, Trev and Dominick told Macy more about ghosts. Only a few people could see them, but not everyone saw ghosts the same way. To some people, they looked alive. Others saw ghosts as shadows or could only feel them as a cold spot in the room. Usually the ability surfaced after a traumatic loss—in Macy's case, probably losing her brother. The three of them traveled around the country, searching for ghosts. They rarely stayed in one place longer than a few months, which seemed really sad to Macy. She couldn't imagine not having her room and her stupid cat who hid under the couch and clawed her ankles when she sat down. And her parents . . . Macy didn't even know if they *had* parents. Or, if they did, if their parents even knew where their children were. Macy didn't even know if Dominick, Trev, and Sam were their real names.

Thinking back on their conversation, Macy

realized she still knew pretty much nothing. She didn't know exactly how the trio "got rid of" the ghosts. Did they vacuum them up like the Ghostbusters? Did they perform some kind of exorcism? And she wasn't even sure why ghosts were dangerous. Trev had said something about ghosts being like jellyfish that had washed up on the beach. Some couldn't hurt you, others stung. But all of them needed to be thrown back into the water. They never once explained Sam's comment about Texas . . .

Sitting in her room, Macy knew she needed to talk to someone or else everything in her head was just going to keep spinning and chewing, spinning and chewing. But she couldn't call Jackson. Calling Jackson would require traveling back to a time before she hated him so much that her stomach acid had burned the words *Jackson is a douche-hat* into the lining of her stomach. Or maybe she was just getting an ulcer.

"How'd it go?" Claire rarely said hello, but just dove right into the conversation. "Did your hands meet in the buttery popcorn? Did you accidentally spill your drink on him and he had to take off his shirt? And then some orphans needed clothes, so he gave them his pants . . . ”

“Uhm, not exactly that.”

Claire always made her smile, even when Macy thought that wasn't possible. When Claire heard that Nick didn't make it, she came right over and talked nonstop about her dad's new girlfriend, who may or may not have been an “adult actress,” and how Claire thought she had accidently walked in on them doing it but they were actually doing yoga together which was almost more disturbing because she was pretty sure they were using her yoga mat, so she donated it to Goodwill the next day. Macy had laughed so hard she thought she was going to throw up. She had to go sit in the bathroom for about ten minutes, leaning over the toilet. But part of that might have been the whiskey she had chugged when her parents weren't looking. It felt good, and then terrible, to swallow the thing that had killed her brother.

"Did you at *least* get to first base?" Claire asked now.

"What does that even mean? Do girls even get on-base?"

"I think first base is over the clothes."

"Did I grope Dominick in the movie theater? Is that what you're asking?" Macy turned on her laptop and waited for it to load. She needed a new computer. Hers had been a gift from "Santa" about five years earlier and it couldn't even play Netflix without crashing.

"Yes. That's exactly what I'm asking."

The computer made a weird grinding sound.

"We made sweet, sweet love at the film festival. In front of all the old people and ushers." Claire once told Macy that she had tried to give one of her boyfriends a hand job at the Opal, but he was too nervous and it didn't work. Macy wasn't sure if that had actually happened. Probably.

"I'm so proud. Little Macy's all grown up. Hey, I gotta go. The mother is making me watch the sister while she goes out and knocks boots."

"Gross."

"Yeah. Bye."

"See ya tomorrow. Bye."

Macy typed in the keywords: *Grey Hills, Washington, Opal, movie theater, murder*. Nothing useful.

Grey Hills, Washington, movie theater, suicide.

She had to scroll through three pages before she found it. Mabel Donati, the daughter of Italian immigrants, was found dead in the Opal two days before Christmas, 1916. An apparent suicide. A single gunshot to the head. There was a picture: the same arching eyebrows and dark lips that made her look like she had stepped out of a black-and-white movie. Mabel had wanted to be an actress.

There was just one small paragraph about her. Nothing that could tell Macy about the kind of life she had lived or why she would have taken her own life. All that was lost.

Macy put away her computer. She lay on the bed and closed her eyes, trying to decide if today had really happened. Was it a dream? She had heard about people who had such vivid dreams that they had trouble remembering if something was a dream or a memory. That wasn't something Macy had ever experienced. Her dreams were usually so weird that there was no mistaking it. Dogs who turned into talking fish. Or she was naked and had to take a math test, but the numbers kept turning into Fruit Loops. After Nick died, Macy dreamed that her teeth kept falling out. Not just one, but all of them at once, crumbling down her chin.

Chapter Nine

Thursday

The sky was a prickly blue as Macy walked to school the next morning. A cold wind cut through her thin jacket and the trees that lined the street shivered and dropped a few leaves. Macy hadn't slept well and her eyes were aching. Her stomach was an acidic pit and she had chewed a handful of cherry-flavored Tums for breakfast. They tasted terrible, like the tampered Halloween candy your parents always warn you about—laced with anti-freeze or something.

As she walked, Macy studied the people on the

street. A woman jogged past. Macy inspected her for bloody wounds. A man pushed a child on a big wheel and she stared at their backs. Could she just make out the shimmer of the harbor through the man's shoulders? No, that was just his leather jacket catching the light.

When she was just a few blocks from school, Macy passed Western Winds. Lorna Evans was sitting on one of the wrought iron benches out front. Macy waved, but Lorna didn't seem to see her. She was probably nearsighted. Macy felt awkward, like she was on the voyeuristic side of a one-way mirror.

It was normally a fifteen-minute walk to school, but Macy spent so long trying to turn her neighbors into ghosts that she had to run the last two blocks from the retirement home to the school, and she was still late for first period—again. Mr. Fitch glanced out of his office as she walked past, but didn't make a move to get up. She probably got a free *dead brother* pass. Nick would have loved that.

Macy was getting used to the empty hallways.

She lingered, looking at a new poster that the seniors had made for the Lock-In. It said *1 DAY,* and the message was drawn to look like it was on fire—red and orange ink licking the black letters. She was surprised the school had let them put that up, especially after Trisha's hair, but maybe the officials hadn't seen it yet. She put her hand over the *1,* imagining she could see the fire through her hand, like when you hold your palm over a light bulb. Then she ripped the poster off the wall and threw it in the trash.

She was almost to English when Jackson grabbed her arm.

"Hey—" Macy began, but he cut her off.

"We're going to talk. Now." He dragged her into a nearby room. Periodic tables on the wall and wide black tables instead of desks. Chemistry. No one used this room during first period, so it was empty. There was a strange, acrid smell in the air—the residue of a failed experiment. Macy's eyes watered.

Jackson's hand on her arm brought Macy back to that day in the basement. Before Jackson tried to kiss her, Macy had never really considered how strong Jackson was. When he had crushed her against the couch, pressing his hand just below her neck, she had felt helpless in a way she never wanted to feel again.

"Let go," she hissed, trying to wrench herself away. He released her arm, but grabbed her by the shoulders.

"You can't just keep walking away from me. Fuck that." Jackson's face was turning red, and his nostrils flared. Knowing Jackson for over a decade, Macy had seen him angry—really, really angry—only a few times. Once, when he was eight, Jackson's mom took away his Nintendo for a week because he broke her reading glasses and then lied about it. Macy knew he had done it because she helped him bury the broken pieces of her glasses in the front yard. Deprived of his Nintendo, Jackson had held his breath for so long that he turned a deep purple and Macy could see the tiny veins on his eyelids. It was pretty scary. She had thought Jackson's head was going to explode.

Now his face was just a few inches from hers— his lips pulled down, showing the tips of his bottom teeth. Even in the basement Macy hadn't felt truly scared, just shocked. But now she could feel his fingers pressing into the bones of her shoulders.

"Jackson," she started, her voice low and thick. "You need to back the fuck off."

"And then what? You'll ignore me again?"

He let go of her but didn't move. Macy backed up until she ran into one of the tables. The door was only about ten feet away. If she ran for it, she could make it. Probably. But this was still Jackson. Would he really hurt her? Most of her said *of course not*, but a tiny, fragile part of her kept repeating *you don't know that, you don't know him anymore.*

Then Jackson's anger seemed to collapse upon itself. He put a hand to his eyes and exhaled a shaky, ragged breath. His face was blotchy, and

Macy realized he might have been crying right before he found her.

"I just want to talk," Jackson said. "I won't touch you." His voice sounded bitter and hurt, but not as angry anymore. Seeing Jackson like this, his shoulders hunched like something newly hatched, Macy sighed. She felt her own anger drain away like a tide flowing back out to sea. It left a hole in its place. The emptiness was worse than the anger. She missed it. At least her anger was something she could control.

"Then talk," she said.

"You saw something Tuesday morning and you need to tell me what. Now. Because I'm seeing things, too." He took a step back, leaning against another table. He had dark circles under his eyes. Macy wondered if he had been sleeping.

"What are you seeing?" Macy didn't recognize her own voice. It sounded flat—almost bored. She licked her lips, and held her arm where he had grabbed her. She was going to have a bruise.

He looked her in the eye as though challenging her to disbelieve him.

"Fire," he said.

That chemical smell was getting stronger and, although it had been cold on the walk to school, it was really hot in the classroom. Macy started sweating. She wiped at the base of her neck, fanning out her shirt. Even her boobs were sweating. Jackson looked flushed, too.

Trev, Sam, and Dominick had talked so easily about ghosts, but it was hard for Macy to form the words. Finally, she said, "I saw a teacher." She paused, looking at the posters on the walls and the little glass beakers on the tabletops, anywhere but Jackson. "He was burning."

Jackson's eyes flashed in confusion, and when he spoke his words were tripping over each other. "A teacher? That wasn't—that's not what I saw. It was just—the air, at the front of class—just for a second. It was on fire. I thought it was all in my head, but then you freaked out. I knew you saw it, too. I knew it." He paused, wiping the back of his neck. "A teacher? Which one?"

Macy closed her eyes. She could still remember Mr. Bishop's deep voice and the poem he had read. *Tyger Tyger, burning bright . . .*

"We don't know him. He was a . . . " Macy felt the word on her tongue before she said it—how round and soft it was. " . . . a ghost."

She opened her eyes expecting to see that *poor Macy actually believes in ghosts* look on Jackson's face. She saw two things instead. First, she saw her friend—the boy she had known for as many years as her memory could hold. There were tears caught in his lower lashes. She felt her heart stutter, as though it had been beating at the wrong frequency and now it was correcting itself. Macy wanted to throw her arms around Jackson—cry into his shirt and tell him how she had missed him all summer: how much it hurt when Nick died and how lost she felt. But what she saw next stopped her.

They weren't alone. The man in gray coveralls stood by the door, dark goggles masking his eyes.

"Come on Jackson," she said. "We should go."

"Are you going to keep ignoring me?" he asked, his voice full of self pity like a child's.

Macy tugged on his arm. "Let's talk about this later. I think he needs the room."

"Who?" Jackson asked, looking around the room.

Macy's blood ran cold. It was an expression she had heard before but had never actually felt until that moment. Even though the room was stuffy and hot, her teeth began to chatter.

"You don't see him?" she whispered, trying to point without actually pointing towards the door. She managed a sort of half-shrug.

"There's no one here."

"Shit, shit, shit." Macy tried to back around the chemistry table, not taking her eyes off the man in the goggles. He smiled widely at her, showing a row of absolutely black teeth—so black it looked like he had been drinking motor oil.

"What, Mace? What's going on?" Jackson turned his head to look where Macy was staring. "I don't see anything." But then he stopped, putting his hand out in front of him. "Fire," he breathed. "I see fire."

The man in the goggles walked toward them. The closer he got, the more Macy noticed just how wrong he looked. His skin had a sheen like an oil-slick. He didn't glow exactly, not the way the woman in the theater did. Where her flesh had captured and filled with light, his skin seemed to repel it. And his clothes were also wrong. Macy now saw that they were covered in tiny blackened holes. It reminded Macy of what happened to her favorite sweatshirt when she had sat too near a bonfire and the little flecks of ash ate through the fabric. In his hand, the man held what Macy now recognized to be a blowtorch.

"God," Macy whispered, hardly realizing that

she was speaking. The man closed the distance between them in the blink of an eye. One instant he was by the door, the next he was standing a few inches away. The smell of him—gasoline and burnt metal—was overpowering. She held her breath. Still grinning, the man grabbed Macy's wrist. The bones and ligaments in her arm felt like they were grinding together.

"Let go," the man whispered, echoing the words Macy had just said to Jackson. His voice was both gravelly and slick, like asphalt melting in the sun. "Let me go." It sounded like he was mocking her.

"Macy?"

She could hear Jackson talking, but he sounded far away. "What's happening?"

Run, she wanted to say. *Run now*. But she couldn't speak. She couldn't look away from the man in the goggles.

The man's grip was so tight that Macy lost feeling in her hand. As her head grew light, she realized that she couldn't see herself in his goggles. They were perfectly black, reflecting nothing.

His grip was no longer just tight, it was scalding. She could feel each of his fingers burning their way into her flesh. The pain was so bright and so sudden that she couldn't even scream.

Then he was gone.

Macy looked to Jackson, who was staring at her burned wrist.

"What the fuck?" he said. "Your arm just . . . "

Her mind struggled to find the words for what had just happened to her, but before she could speak, the piercing ring of the school fire alarm filled the room.

Chapter Ten

Macy and Jackson ran out of the room, joining the mass of students walking quickly down the hall toward the front door. Teachers led them out to the courtyard where they waited for fire trucks to arrive. Macy heard someone say it wasn't a drill, but she already knew that because it was her fucking burned skin that had probably set off the alarms.

The pain from Macy's wrist was making her stomach queasy, but she didn't know what to do about it. How would she explain how she got a burn—let alone a burn in the exact shape of a hand? They would blame her for the fire alarm, thinking she had burned herself . . . but how? Everyone would think she was crazy.

Jackson left her standing beneath one of the ornamental cherry trees that decorated the front of the school. A leaf fell in her hair and it felt like a spider. Even though she knew Jackson had told her where he was going, she couldn't remember. She could only feel the white, sickening pain of her wrist.

"Macy?" Dom appeared before her. "Hey, I just wanted to talk to you about last night. I know it was a lot to take in and . . . " his voice trailed off. "Are you okay?"

At first, she nodded, then she shook her head. She wiped away a tear, but fuck that—she was not going to cry.

"Oh my God! Your arm! What happened?"

"I don't know," she croaked, angling her arm away from Dom. She didn't want him to see the hand-shaped burn because then she'd have to talk about it, and right now she couldn't even speak.

Macy tried to cover her wrist with her other hand, but it hurt too much.

"Is that a burn?" Dom asked. "Shit, it looks bad. I'll get a teacher."

"No!" She reached out and grabbed the hem of his shirt with her good hand, pulling him back. Before she let go, she caught a glimpse of his hip and the tan skin of his lower back.

"What's going on? I can help."

Macy kept shaking her head. She still didn't know what had happened to her. She just wanted everything to go away.

When Jackson returned, he was holding two Cokes from the vending machine. "Here. It's cold." He tried to press one of the bottles against her wrist.

Macy moved her arm away from him. "Don't. It hurts."

"Well, no shit, 'it hurts'—that's what the Coke is for. It's cold," he repeated.

"Don't."

Dominick turned on Jackson. "Did you do this to her?"

"Who are you?"

Dominick asked Macy this time. "Did he hurt you? I'll call the cops."

"Who the fuck are you?" Jackson stood up to his full height.

"Who the fuck are *you*?"

Dominick was inches away from Jackson, but only eye-level with his collarbone. Jackson held up the Cokes like they were the weapons of a forgotten Ninja Turtle who fought with pop bottles instead of nunchucks. Macy would have laughed if she wasn't pretty sure that her skin was peeling off. Oh yeah, and a fucking ghost had just grabbed her arm. Could ghosts do that? They didn't even have bodies, did they?

"Dom, this is my friend Jackson. He didn't hurt me. I got burned by . . . " She wasn't sure what to say. "Something. Like, what you showed me yesterday."

Dom glanced at Jackson again. "Did he see it?"

"Sort of . . . Not exactly." She blinked back tears. "Does it matter? It fucking burned me. With its hand."

Sirens filled the air. A fire truck, ambulance, and two cop cars pulled up in front of the school.

"What should I do?" Macy tried to cover her arm again. "They're here for me."

"Were you in the kitchen?" Dom asked.

"No. The chemistry room. What does the kitchen have to do with anything?"

"I heard there was a grease fire in the kitchen. It was huge. Do you want me to go get a paramedic?" In the morning light, Dom's face looked younger than it had the night before. His jaw seemed softer, the scar on his chin wasn't that noticeable. He held her gaze for a long moment as though waiting for directions.

The moment was interrupted by Jackson opening one of the Cokes. He took a long swallow, draining half the bottle.

"What?" he asked when Macy stared at him. "Did you want it? You can still have the other one."

She shook her head, then noticed the crowd of students closest to the front door moving off the walkway onto the grass. Mr. Fitch directed them, pointing at some students and gently moving others with his big hands. Some kids still gathered around the walkway, trying to get a glimpse of whoever was being wheeled out on a gurney.

There was an oxygen mask covering her face. Macy could tell it was a woman by the few strands of brown hair that hung off the side of the gurney and her bright pink shoes. But she wasn't close enough to tell if she knew the person. Before they closed the ambulance doors, Macy saw the woman's bare legs—red and blistered. Macy's empty stomach turned.

"Can we go?" she asked, already taking a few steps back away from the ambulance, and the woman on the stretcher.

Jackson said something about taking her to a

hospital, but Macy couldn't concentrate on his voice. The grass was damp and the dew soaked into her shoes. She wondered how it would feel to press her burned arm against the grass. Would the grass stick to her arm or would pieces of her skin stick to the grass?

"Wait," Dom said. "Just wait a minute." He was staring at something past the ambulance that was already pulling away, siren blasting. Past the students. "Look—do you see her? That woman—right there?"

A woman with long brown hair stood by the kitchen windows at the front of the school. Macy recognized her from the lunch line, but she had never learned her name. She was wearing a blue dress and a white apron. Her arms were crossed over her chest as she watched a policeman write notes on a little white pad.

"What am I looking for?"

"Look at her legs. Keep looking."

With a sinking feeling, Macy stared at the

woman's bare legs. She didn't blink, even when her eyes started to sting. They were nice legs: thin but muscular, with that line down the calf that women wore high heels to achieve. Macy sometimes looked at her own legs in the mirror—flexing and relaxing them just to see that line. Then Macy noticed her shoes. They were pink.

The woman's legs began to turn red. Blisters formed, worse than the sunburn Macy got one summer when she fell asleep on the beach and the skin on her back started peeling off in silver dollar-sized chunks. Much worse than the burn on her wrist now.

"Oh." Macy had no words for what she was seeing. The blisters traveled up the woman's body, covering her arms, her face.

"I don't see anything," Jackson said, but Macy ignored him. She couldn't look away from the burning woman.

"She doesn't realize she's dead yet," Dominick

said. "When she figures it out, she probably won't stay for long. Most don't."

"Is she a ghost, then? Like the woman in the theater?"

"Sort of. More like an after-image. Ghosts, the kind we usually deal with—they're the ones who stay."

Even as he spoke, the woman changed. She looked down at herself, taking in her burnt legs and ruined arms. Then she looked up to the sky and began to fade. It was like watching a Polaroid develop in reverse. First, she began to lose color, the blue of her dress becoming a flat gray, her brown hair turning black. Then, her edges grew softer, her fingers losing focus, legs blurring. The faint pink of her shoes blended with the green of the grass. The woman just stared into the bright blue of the sky. When there was only a trace of her left—the barest outline of her shoulders, the curve of her head— Macy blinked, and then the woman was gone.

Macy got into the back of Dominick's car. It smelled like cigarettes, and the seat had dark stains wide as continents on a map. Jackson sat in back, too, even though his long legs didn't really fit, and it made Dominick look like a chauffeur all alone in the front.

He drove toward the bluffs, winding through narrow residential roads, the pavement cracked by tree roots. Macy held her injured arm right next to the burned area—digging her fingernails into her skin every time they went over a bump. The burn was getting darker every minute, reminding Macy of the red handprints on Indian War ponies in old Western movies. Jackson put his hand on her shoulder but she shrugged him off. Her skin was electric.

Dom pulled up to one of the old Victorian houses. It was a dull yellow with white trim that reminded Macy of a lemon meringue pie. One of the windows was broken and taped up with a plastic sheet.

Dom opened Macy's door for her. "Home sweet home."

"You live here?"

"I hope so. This is the address I've been giving the pizza guy."

Macy surprised herself by laughing. Jackson rolled his eyes. "Can we focus on Macy's arm? She might have third-degree burns."

Dom shrugged, unlocking the front door. "Sure thing, doc."

Inside, the house had obviously been remodeled. The hardwood floor had a polished sheen and the walls looked freshly painted. Dom led them towards the kitchen to get ice. They walked past a living room that was empty except for two camping chairs. The air smelled like burnt toast and cigarettes.

"Dom?" Trev yelled from upstairs. "You home?

I thought you weren't going to be a lazy truant like me and Sam."

Trev walked down a set of stairs near the kitchen. He only had on a pair of blue boxers and Macy could see how freckled his shoulders and arms were. His hair was sticking up, but not in the styled way Macy had seen before. "Oh, you've brought Macy and . . . friend."

Trev was wearing glasses—he must have worn contacts before—and his eyes were bloodshot. Macy could smell alcohol wafting off him like he was a flambé.

"Macy's burned. Do we have an icepack or something?"

Sam walked in from another room. She was carrying a book in one hand, and a mug in the other. Her long, wet hair darkened her tank top across an obviously braless chest. Macy could tell that Jackson was trying not to stare at Sam's boobs, but she was in too much pain to feel embarrassed for him.

"Are we having a party?" Sam asked, taking a sip of her coffee.

"Sam, something really bad happened at school," Dom said.

"Did you see your shadow? Are we having four more weeks of winter?"

Dom acted like he didn't hear her and told them about the fire at school and Macy's arm. "She says it was a ghost that grabbed her."

"You poor thing—let me see." Sam led Macy into the kitchen. It was full of sunlight, with a huge glass door that led out to an obviously neglected garden. Beyond the garden was the bright sheen of the water. The beauty of the room was marred by the dirty dishes that covered the countertop and filled the sink. "It actually doesn't look that bad. Here, let's run some cold water over it."

Sam started clearing dishes out of the sink. "Trev! Get your shit out of the sink. Fucking pig."

"It's your shit too." Trev reappeared with a shirt

on and helped move bowls and plates to already full counters.

"Don't you guys have a dishwasher?" Jackson asked.

"Yeah," Sam smiled. "Dom." She turned on the water and the cold made Macy gasp in relief. "Hold still, sweetie. It's really not so bad. Looks much worse than it is."

"Thanks." Macy's teeth chattered. She didn't like being called *sweetie* and hadn't forgotten the slap Sam gave her on the beach, but she also remembered Sam's coat, which Macy still hadn't returned. Sam didn't let go of her hand while the water numbed the burn, and Macy noticed how ragged Sam's nails were and how she had freckles on her arms just like her brother.

After Sam bandaged Macy's arm and gave her two aspirin, like the internet had told them to, they all sat down around an old wooden table. It was one of the few pieces of real furniture that Macy had seen in the house. Macy introduced Jackson to the others, and then Dom pulled up a map on his laptop. It looked a lot like a Google Map of the U.S., but with a few strange black markers scattered across the screen.

"What is it?"

"A map of the dead."

"No shit?" Jackson said. Macy stared at the markers. They looked like those characters on that old Pac Man game. The ghosts.

"So you just travel around looking for ghosts?" Jackson sounded deeply skeptical, but Macy knew that was for show. He tapped his foot loudly on the hardwood floor, which he always did when he was nervous.

"Sort of. We find ghosts, but we're looking for something else. We call them Doors."

"A door?" Macy asked.

"Door to the Dead. Ghosts can pass through them. That's one way that they end up here."

"They use them like a fucking highway," Trev said.

Macy took the mouse and focused the map on Washington, near Grey Hills. "Where's our Door?"

"That's the question." Dom sounded like the eager teacher whose student was actually participating in class. "Where's your Door? You see, there's actually a pattern to the Doors."

"You think," said Sam. She had gotten up and opened the fridge. The cold air made the hair on the back of Macy's neck stand up.

"Yes, I think," Dom continued. "I'm pretty sure. And shut the fridge, you're letting all the cold out."

"Okay, mom." Sam pulled out a few beers before slamming the door shut. "Who wants one?"

"It's 8:30 in the morning."

Macy reached out with her good arm. "I'll take one." Sam opened the cap and handed it to her. The first sip was so cold her tongue tingled. Jackson went to grab it from Macy, but she pulled the bottle out of his reach.

Sam held a beer in front of her brother's face. "Hair of the dog?"

Trev groaned, pushing it away. "Hair of the fuck you."

"So," Macy couldn't help but ask. "Why do you look like hell?"

Trev took off his glasses and rubbed his eyes again. "Late night. Research."

Dominick held up air quotes. "Oh yeah, *research*. He was researching how much rum a person can drink before they pass out on the toilet."

"Research and *allergies*," Trev amended. "I'm allergic to mornings."

"Eight shots of rum. I think that was the scientific conclusion. Or was it nine? I lost count after you took off your pants."

Trev held up his middle finger.

"You were saying about the Doors?" Jackson said. "Doors, like, actual doors? We can just walk through them and end up in, like, Ghostland or something?"

"Yeah," Trev said, just as Dom said, "Not really."

Sam handed Jackson a beer. "Jackson, huh? Who did you lose?"

"What?"

"If you can see things—like we can—then someone died. Who was it?"

Macy looked over at her friend. She could actually see Jackson's face change—his lips pressed together, small blotches of red appearing on his cheeks.

"My mom."

"That'd do it. And, sorry."

Macy thought Sam might tell them who she and Trev had lost, but she just took a long drink of her beer, then held the bottle to her forehead.

"Anyway," Dominick continued. "You can see this big gap here, over Washington. There should be a Door somewhere in this region."

"Or there never was a pattern," Sam said. "And the Doors are randomly scattered."

"I'm sorry, I don't really understand," Jackson said. "They're, like, real doors? With doorknobs?"

The more Macy looked at the computer screen, the more it felt like she was on one of those pirate ship carnival rides and her whole world was listing. Her wrist still hurt like a bitch, even if the burn wasn't as bad as she had thought.

Sam sighed. "Why are we even showing them this?"

"We can use their help." Dom pointed at the map. "They might know something about the area. Something we've overlooked."

"Maybe. If you're right."

"Right about what?" Macy asked. It almost felt like she was back watching that terrible French movie—like everyone else was speaking another language and she had missed the subtitles. "About doors? Ghosts?"

Sam and Dom both looked at each other—a kind of stalemate. It was Trev who spoke.

"How much do you know about the Fire?"

Then, because he wasn't from Grey Hills, he added, "The one that happened fifty years ago?"

Chapter Eleven

Macy had always known about the Fire. Growing up in Grey Hills meant that you absorbed the story of the Fire along with the salt wind and the call of seagulls near the harbor. She knew, for example, that it was an accident. That there was a storm and some kind of electrical problem—maybe lightning struck the power lines, or a tree fell. Something dramatic and unstoppable. An act of God.

How did the fire spread so quickly? Why didn't the doors open? Why were so many students trapped inside as the walls burned and the roof bloomed sparks and flame, and then collapsed? These were not questions Macy had really considered before.

The Fire happened. It was a fact. As solid and unchangeable as a constellation and as familiar as the orange poppies that grew along the bottom of the bluffs.

"But aren't there rumors?" Trev asked. "Don't they say something else was going on? That maybe it wasn't an accident?"

"I guess," Jackson answered. "You always hear things."

Sam had finished her beer and started peeling off the label in thin strips. "What kinds of things?" She slipped each strip into the bottle itself, like she was going to send out a message in it.

"The principal started the fire. Or one of the students. Or there was a curse on the school—Indian burial ground kind of stuff."

"What do you think happened?" Dom asked, looking at Macy.

"What did I used to think, or what do I think now?"

"Both, I suppose."

"Well, I never used to think about it. I guess I just figured it was some shitty accident—lightning or something. But now? Come on. Look at my arm."

"You think a ghost did it?"

"Isn't that why we're talking about it? A ghost with a blowtorch? And someone just died today." Macy drank the last sip of her beer. It had grown warm and made her tongue pucker.

Dom shook his head. "Ghosts can't really do things like that—start fires. Not by themselves at least. That's not how it works."

"Can you lend me your manual on ghosts? I seem to have lost mine when a ghost burned my arm with its fucking hand."

Sam removed Macy's empty bottle and set another in front of her. Macy set her fingertips on the cold glass. "I don't know if I should have another."

Trev's voice was muffled when he said, "You

definitely should." He had his head cradled in his arms.

Macy put the bottle to her lips. She had never been drunk on a school day, let alone before third period.

"Ghosts aren't that strong," Dom continued.

"Some are," Sam said. "Remember Texas?" The strips of paper inside Sam's bottle had begun to resemble a plant.

"Yes. Some are," Dom conceded. "But those are special cases. Most of the ghosts we've seen can't even touch you."

Macy held up her arm. "This one can." The beer was making her sleepy. She wanted to lean her head against Jackson's shoulder. Instead, she checked her phone. Two missed calls from Claire, and a text: *Where are you?* She wrote back, *Home.* Macy didn't want to lie to her friend, but there was no place for Claire in her head.

"Then why do you get rid of them?" Jackson asked.

"Because," Trev said, propping up his head with his hand. "Ghosts shouldn't be here. It isn't natural."

"We don't know that," Dominick said softly.

"We don't?" Jackson asked. He had hardly touched his beer and kept looking out the window as though he expected a ghost to pop up, like on a haunted house carnival ride.

"Dom, stop it," Trev said.

"But we don't know. How can we know what's *natural,* as you put it? How can we know that they aren't supposed to be here?"

"I don't want to talk about this now. It never goes anywhere and my head feels like an elephant's shitting on my brain."

"Fine. But I still don't think a ghost could have caused the Fire. I never thought that."

"So that's really why you're here?" Macy asked, "To solve the *great mystery* of the Fire?"

"Well, we're not here to take math tests," Sam said. "And we're sure as shit not here to deal with one popcorn-munching ghost. We're here because of the Fire."

"Because of the Door," Dominick clarified. "There should be a Door here. We think the Fire in 1966 was a ritual that went wrong. A ritual that was supposed to open the Door. Here's the thing. Ghosts are like shadows most of the time. Like that teacher, Mr. Bishop. He was barely there."

Macy shook her head. "He was there. I could hear him screaming." She was already halfway done with her second beer. This one tasted better—like bread and flowers.

"Remember when I said the woman earlier was like an after-image?" Dom said. "Mr. Bishop wasn't really there—not all of him. He was just caught in a loop—enacting how he died over and over again. I stopped the loop."

"How?" Macy remembered the way Dom had closed his eyes and gripped the edge of the desk.

"It's hard to explain. I just imagined him dissolving. At peace."

"You wished him gone? Like, clapping your hands and saying, 'I do believe in fairies'?"

"Yeah, Dom," Sam said, lifting up her bottle to inspect her handiwork. "You just think happy thoughts?"

Macy wondered if there was something between Sam and Dom. Each time Macy had seen them together, Sam had been pretty nasty to him. Did they used to date or something? Macy tried not to think about Dom's hands in Sam's hair. Her braless chest.

Dom explained briefly how ghosts were really just psychic energy and you can disrupt that energy with enough concentration. "But," he concluded. "It takes a long time to learn."

"Most of us go the old-fashioned route," Sam said. "You stab them in the face."

Macy and Jackson both stared at her. "What?"

"Not always the face. The neck works. Or the chest, but sometimes they forget they had a heart and don't get the message."

Trev lifted his head from the table again. "What Sam is trying to say is that there are several ways to concentrate your own psychic energy, as Dom puts it. Some of us need something to focus on. A knife, for example."

"So you can kill a ghost?"

"Kind of," Sam said. "They sometimes forget that they're dead. A knife to the face really reminds them."

Dom cleared his throat. "Knives aren't necessary. But people have always found ways to focus their energy. A cross is one way. Fire is another."

Macy rubbed her bandaged wrist. "Fire?"

"Like I said before, I think that the Fire in 1966 was a ritual—a way to focus someone's energy. They started a fire—maybe using that ghost—and killed people to open a Door. Death also releases a lot of energy."

"But it didn't work?"

"No. That's why I think someone might be about to try it again."

"So all those fires at the school? The ghost? They're all part of some ritual?"

"They could be. That's what we need to find out. If we can link Macy's ghost to the fifty-year-old fire, then we might be able to figure it out."

"My ghost?" Thinking of the ghost with the goggles as *hers* made her feel like centipedes were crawling up her arms.

"Wait," Jackson asked. "How exactly does someone use a ghost?" Macy wondered if Jackson actually believed anything Dom was saying. She wouldn't blame him if he didn't. Macy could hardly believe it, and she had a ghost's fingerprints branded on her skin.

"You need a Token. An object that belonged to the ghost when he was alive. Something special. This could be a favorite watch, or one of his bones."

"That's what she said." Trev's face was once again pressed into the crook of his arm.

Dom glared but kept talking. "Bones are actually

a really powerful link to the dead. Bones, blood, and hair all make great Tokens."

Jackson took another small sip of his beer, then asked, "Do you have a suspect? Anyone who was alive during the Fire is probably dead by now, right?"

"Actually," Trev sat up again, rubbing his eyes. "We do have someone in mind. What do you think of Mr. Fitch?"

Macy remembered his kind words the day before, and his dead sister. "I hardly know him."

"Think about it. Mr. Fitch came to town almost exactly fifty years after the school fire. Wasn't the Fire in early September?"

Jackson and Macy nodded.

"September 9th," Dom clarified. "Fifty years ago tomorrow."

"Tomorrow's the Lock-In," Macy mumbled, realizing they'd probably cancel it anyway after the kitchen fire.

"Well," Trev continued. "Mr. Fitch arrives at

the school and there are immediately two fires. And he's related to the principal who actually died in the Fire. What if Principal Grey was behind the first fire, and Vice Principal Fitch is picking up where his grandpa left off? Makes sense, right?"

"Maybe," said Sam. "Or maybe the Fire really was an accident. And this ghost of Macy's has nothing to do with it." Sam's hair was so long that the ends pooled on the tabletop. Her hair had started to frizz around the top of her head as it dried and glowed in the sunlight. Macy realized that Sam wasn't wearing makeup. Her lashes were naturally blonde. There was a pockmark just above her eyebrow that she must usually cover with foundation. Macy again wondered about her and Dom—had he ever kissed that pockmark?

"I don't know," Macy said. "Why would Mr. Fitch do it? Why would anyone do it?"

"That's what we need to find out," Dom said. "Because if someone is trying to recreate the ritual, then for all we know the date is as important as the Fire. We may only have one day to stop him."

"If there *is* a ritual. And if it *is* Mr. Fitch," Sam said.

Dom ignored her. "It's too bad it was so long ago. What we need is to talk to someone who was there. Find out what really happened."

For the first time that day, Macy knew exactly what to do.

Macy found Lorna in the Western Winds lobby, reading in a plush chair beside the empty fireplace. Even though she wasn't technically volunteering, Macy got herself a free cup of coffee and then sat down next to Lorna.

"Hello. Beautiful day, isn't it?" Macy set her coffee on the table in front of them.

Lorna lowered her book, *Jane Eyre*, but didn't quite set it down. "I haven't really been outside yet." The older woman peered at Macy. "Isn't it a school day?"

"It is, but they let us out early." Macy didn't mention the kitchen fire—she didn't want to upset Lorna right before asking her about *the* Fire. "I actually have a favor to ask you."

"Me? How can I help you?"

"Well, I'm writing a paper for History."

"Oh," Lorna put down her book. "Did you know that I used to be a history teacher?"

"Really?" Macy grinned. "History is my favorite subject."

"I was a teacher for almost thirty years." Lorna looked like she was going to say something else, but then closed her mouth, pressing her lips together.

"Well, I was actually wondering if you could help me out. Like I said, I'm writing a paper. I'm writing about the Fire."

"I see." Lorna frowned—just a slight furrowing of her brows and an almost imperceptible turning down of her lips. But it was enough to make Macy feel bad for mentioning it.

"We're supposed to interview people. It's called a primary source. I was wondering . . . could you tell me about it? That day? Anything would help."

Lorna no longer met Macy's eyes, but was looking somewhere beyond her. She kept touching her whalebone bracelet—turning it around and around on her wrist. "Are you sure your teacher wants you to write about this? It was a horrible thing. Just horrible."

Macy nodded, not trusting her voice. She hated making Lorna relive something so awful.

"I suppose I can try, but it really was such a long time ago."

"Thank you so much. Like I said, anything would help." Macy took out her laptop, cringing as it grinded to life. She signed into Skype, and IM'd Dom: *Ready.* Then she took out her phone. "Is it okay if I tape our conversation? The teacher suggested recording it so we can review it later."

"All right, I suppose."

"I'll just use my phone to record." Macy pressed Dom's number, which she had just put in her contact list before leaving the big yellow house. When he picked up, she put it on speakerphone and set it on the table between her and Lorna.

"What can you tell me about the Fire?"

Lorna twisted her bracelet again. "As I said, it was just horrible."

Macy waited, but Lorna didn't continue. Dom skyped another question for her: *What can you tell me about the morning of the Fire?*

Lorna thought for a moment. "It was raining. It took us all by surprise—the skies just opened up on the drive to school. I remember that I didn't have my raincoat with me. All of the children were cranky, especially the boys because they were worried that the football game might be cancelled because of the storm. They were so young . . . " She paused, and Macy worried that she might start crying, but her eyes were dry. "I remember I was talking about World War II that day. It wasn't that long ago then—some of the students had parents who had fought in the war. But all they wanted to talk about was Vietnam. They didn't understand how it felt—to be in a just war. To know that your whole country is fighting evil. They didn't understand."

Another question from Dom: *Do you know how the fire started?*

"They told us it was lightning—it struck the school. I think that's right. The storm was like nothing I'd ever seen."

"Did you see anything else unusual that day? Were there any strangers at school?"

"I'm not sure what you're asking. There was nothing strange. Just a storm."

"Of course—I just have this list of questions. Sorry. Just a few more." Macy smiled at her, which suddenly felt completely inappropriate so she looked back to her computer. "Were you close to the fire before you got out?" Macy asked the question before realizing that Dom couldn't see Lorna's scars. She tried to avoid looking at Lorna's arm, the shiny scars on the side of her neck.

"Yes. I was very close," Lorna twisted her bracelet again and again. Macy hoped she wouldn't break it. "I think the Fire started in the afternoon. It was so dark from the storm that it could have been evening. The alarms didn't go off. I was talking to the class and then the door opened and the flames poured in. I think the fire pushed it open. The children were screaming . . . "

Macy wanted to stop, but she asked Dom's next question: *How did you get out?*

It was a long moment before Lorna spoke again. "I broke a window." Then Lorna closed her eyes and didn't say anything for a long while. When the old woman met Macy's eyes again, she said, "Do you have everything? I can't imagine you need to know all of this for a paper."

"Yes," Macy closed her laptop, and ended the

call to Dom. "Thanks so much! I think this is exactly what my teacher wanted."

"I hope so. You're a good student, aren't you, Macy?"

"Yes, I try to be."

"I heard you just lost your brother. Nick, wasn't it? I'm so sorry."

Macy didn't know what to say, so she just nodded.

"Your poor parents. How terrible, to lose a child."

"Do you have children?" Macy asked, trying to change the subject. She couldn't actually remember anyone coming to visit Lorna, at least while she was volunteering.

Lorna shook her head. "No. No children. But I have my books." She gave a slight smile, and held up the book she had been reading—her hand still marking her page.

Jesus. How lonely she must be.

Macy smiled. "Well, I'll let you get back to your reading—it must be a good one."

"When you're finished, I'd like to read what you wrote," Lorna said, peering over the top of her book. "I can help you."

"That would be great," Macy said as she packed up her computer. She wondered if this meant that she actually had to write the paper.

Chapter Twelve

Friday

Everyone ate in the gym: sack lunches with a sandwich, apple, cookie, and bag of chips. Apparently there was no real damage to the kitchen itself—just a burned pan and some superficial staining to the stove and cabinets from the smoke. But the school must have thought it would be in poor taste, so to speak, to serve food where a woman had just died. Macy wondered how thoroughly they had cleaned the kitchen and if there were bits of Miss Henderson (that was the lunch lady's name) still floating in the air.

There weren't quite enough tables. Some of the freshmen were sitting in the corner of the gym by the bleachers, while others sat beneath a basketball hoop—making the room resemble a disaster relief effort. If Claire was surprised when Jackson sat at their table, she didn't say anything.

"This is not enough food," Sam said, dumping the contents of her bag onto the table. Her apple rolled off the edge, but she caught it before it hit the floor. Trev pulled apart the bread of his sandwich. "I got tuna. Is that even legal?"

"I'll trade you for my ham if you'll stop whining." Dom swapped bags with Trev, who looked much improved from the day before. Trev's face no longer had that slightly green tinge, which had clashed with his hair.

Jackson looked in his bag. "This sucks, I got two apples and no cookie."

"Take mine, I wasn't going to eat it anyway." Claire hadn't spoken to Jackson all summer in solidarity to Macy, but as she handed him her oatmeal raisin cookie, it was like nothing had happened. She must have just been waiting for them to make up. "By the way, so weird that we're still having the Lock-In tonight, right? I mean, is it even going to be fun?"

"We are?" Macy asked.

Claire nodded. "Yeah—didn't your first period teacher say anything? Mom said that they were going to cancel it, but then Mr. Fitch argued for it. He said that if we could have school today, then we could still do the Lock-In. My mom thinks it's really weird."

"So he's a champion of the people, huh?" Trev said through a mouthful of ham and cheese. "Standing up for our God-given right to sleep on the ground in musty sleeping bags."

Macy couldn't remember much about first period. Mrs. Polly had said something about the senseless accident, but she didn't mention the way the lunch lady's clothes had burned onto her skin, or how she had actually lived through the fire only to die as the paramedics moved her to the ambulance. Nobody talked about the things that mattered.

"I don't think I'll go," Macy said, picking at the bandage on her wrist. When Claire first saw her injured arm that morning, she had taken Macy aside and demanded to know if she had hurt herself. Like, on purpose. Macy had tried to cut herself once, a few days after Nick died. She had only told Claire about it because it was so dumb—holding a butter knife to her palm. That wasn't even the right kind of knife and she had only managed a shallow scrape that had barely bled. It wasn't that she had really wanted to hurt herself. She had just wondered if it would help. Nothing helped.

When Claire asked about her hurt wrist, Macy had laughed and told Claire that she burned herself making dinner. But she knew it sounded like a lie because she *was* lying. Claire kept giving her these long looks while they ate, with her dark, neatly plucked eyebrows arched like the tops of question marks.

Claire frowned. "You've been looking forward to this for years. I think you should come." She was pretty sure Claire just didn't want her to be alone. Macy wondered again if she should just tell Claire everything. But . . . Claire would never believe her. How could she even begin to explain, anyway?

"Yeah," Sam said. "We're all going." She crumpled up her paper bag and threw it at her brother's head. It missed and almost hit Jackson, who didn't look like he minded.

"Come on, Mace." It sounded strange to hear Trev call her by her nickname.

Dom added, "It won't be the same without you." Which really meant that they still wanted her help to snoop around the school for clues like they were in some fucking Nancy Drew mystery.

Macy looked to Jackson to see if he was going to try to badger her into going, too. He shook his head. "I think Macy should do whatever she wants." He took a big bite of his apple, then spit it out. "It's all mealy. Do you want it?" He held it out for Claire, but she ignored him.

Macy almost hadn't come to school, but Dom and Trev wanted her there so she could tell them if she saw anything out of the ordinary. She was the only one, after all, who had seen the ghost. All Jackson had seen, from his rather vague descriptions, was *fire*. Dom had said that they'd protect her if the ghost came back, though she wasn't sure how he planned to do that when he wasn't in all of her classes and the ghost could literally burn someone's face off. But looking for the ghost wasn't what made her return to school.

For the past few days, Macy had been nurturing a small, almost microscopic hope that maybe, just maybe, she would see her brother.

The night before, after coming home from Dominick's house late (she told her parents that she had been at Claire's), she had opened Nick's door. He never let her go in his room when he was alive, but he couldn't do a fucking thing about it now that he was dead. She lay down on his bed and pressed her face into his pillow. She tried to be quiet so her parents wouldn't hear. Macy had inhaled the smell of her brother, thinking how she might be breathing in bits of him—skin cells, atoms. Her mother hadn't cleaned his room since his accident, hadn't touched a single thing. Nick's water glass was still on the side table—three dead fruit flies sunk to the bottom. A stray brown hair lay on the sheet next to her head.

Some of his things were in boxes, but that was because he had already started packing for college. He always did things way too early. Nick *should have* been getting ready to leave for the University of Washington. Macy was going to get his car after he left, because he wouldn't need it in the city. He told her, in a rare instance of brotherly affection, that she could come visit him at school some weekend. Take the ferry, then the bus to the U-District. She could sleep on his floor. Do her homework in some trendy coffee shop where college guys might mistake her for a freshman.

Instead, Nick destroyed her car. He had been dead for over three weeks. They hadn't even had a funeral for him yet. Her mom said that it took time to plan a funeral, but Macy was pretty sure that her parents just didn't want to say goodbye.

All morning at school Macy had literally kept looking over her shoulder, expecting to see those dark goggles, that horrible black smile. But she also looked for her brother.

After lunch, as she walked to Calculus, Macy noticed a new poster on the wall. It said: 0 DAYS. The letters weren't burning this time. They were plain red on a black background. Black as the ghost's teeth.

Chapter Thirteen

Around eight-ish, Macy's mom dropped her and Claire off at the school. "Try to get some sleep," her mom said as she helped them get their things out of the trunk. "I'll be back at eight tomorrow morning."

When it was just Macy and her mom in the car, right before they picked up Claire, Macy had almost told her mom to stop. That she didn't want to go to the Lock-In after all. Macy had been thinking about what Lorna had said during their interview: how terrible it was to lose a child. What would her parents do if something went wrong tonight and they lost her too? Could they survive that? Macy watched her mom drive, memorizing the line of her jaw, the curl of brown hair that she tucked behind her ear. The little worry lines around her mother's mouth. In the end, Macy didn't say anything and the car kept moving forward.

As they walked toward the gym, Macy's backpack—containing a toothbrush, toothpaste, pajamas, and her retainer (which she was not going to let anyone see)—was slung over one shoulder. She carried her sleeping bag in front of her like a shield. It was actually her brother's blue Coleman sleeping bag, because hers was almost ten years old and was pink with a My Little Pony pattern. The sleeping bag didn't smell like her brother, but like the garage, which made it easier somehow.

The lunchroom was still closed off, so the juniors and seniors congregated in the gym where pizza and bowls of early Halloween candy were spread out on tables. There were also board games like Monopoly and Apples to Apples. Students stood around, trying to decide where to put their pillows and sleeping bags. Some people were already wearing pajamas—flannel pants and tank-tops—but Macy was still in jeans. She didn't think she would be sleeping tonight.

"Wow, killer party," Sam said, rolling her eyes. She and her brother had already staked out a corner by the door to the locker rooms and were standing next to a large, black duffel bag. Dom leaned against the wall next to Sam. Jackson had been hovering a little off to the side away from Dom. He waved when Macy and Claire came in and moved closer to the group.

Claire pointed toward the twin's duffel bag, "What on earth did you bring? A dead body?"

Trev grinned. "Can't a guy have a few secrets?"

Macy caught Dom's eye. She wondered if he was as nervous as she was. She also wondered what Sam and Trev had brought—some kind of ghost repellent, she hoped.

Someone turned on the music and a thumping beat echoed softly through the gym. The chaperones hadn't left yet and were standing by the food table. Mr. Fitch chewed on a slice of pepperoni pizza.

"See," Dominick whispered to Macy, pointing at the vice principal. "He made sure he was one of the chaperones." If Dominick and Trev were right, then Mr. Fitch was going to make his pet ghost burn the school to the ground tonight. It sounded ridiculous. There was no other word for it. Picturing balding, beer-bellied Mr. Fitch as some evil mastermind—it was just laughable. Macy still didn't know if she believed in the ritual. Sam sure didn't seem to, but there was no denying the ghost. Watching the students rolling out sleeping bags, Macy couldn't help but imagine them trapped and screaming while the building burned around them.

"Where do you guys want to sleep?" Claire asked. Her hair was in two thin braids and she was wearing light blue pajamas pants with little stars and crescent moons on them. They ended up spreading out their sleeping bags in a circle with their heads facing in as though around a campfire. Claire made sure her bag was between Macy and Trev's, and she stopped Jackson from taking the spot on the other side of Macy so Dominick could sleep there. Not that Macy could possibly sleep anyway, but thinking about waking up next to Dominick gave her stomach a momentary flutter.

The first few hours were actually pretty fun in a third-grade-sleepover kind of way. Claire wanted to play Apples to Apples. Trev had brought a few bottles of "iced tea," a sip of which made Macy's eyes water. After the chaperones left to go hang out in the teacher's lounge, or some other part of the school, a few students started dancing. Someone threw a dodge ball back and forth over the top of the dancers. The pizza was cold and greasy by then, though Sam still ate two-and-a-half pieces. The half was because her brother took her unfinished slice and whipped it at Dom's head when he wasn't looking. Macy couldn't stomach the congealed cheese and ended up eating several handfuls of fun-sized snickers bars instead.

Eventually Dominick leaned over and whispered in Macy's ear: "Let's go explore." She nodded, but blushed at the look Claire gave her as she snuck out of the gym holding Dominick's hand. First stop was Mr. Fitch's office. Dom kept almost turning the wrong way, and Macy had to tug on his shirt and point. They weren't using flashlights and tried to be quiet in case the chaperones were around.

It wasn't nearly as dark as she thought it would be. There were some small safety lights spaced evenly throughout the hallway illuminating the school in a soft, bluish glow. Her shadow puddled around her feet and she was so aware of the empty hallway behind her that the air seemed to buzz.

When they finally found Mr. Fitch's office, the door was locked. Macy expected Dom to pull out a bobby pin or something and pick the lock, but he just stood there, his hand pressed to the glass window on the door.

"Shit," he whispered.

"You didn't think it would be locked? Of course it's locked. It's probably school policy."

"Shit," he whispered again. "Maybe we should call Sam?"

Macy could see her reflection in the glass as she stood behind Dom. The shadows made her eyes look huge, the rest of her face skeletal. She looked fierce.

"No. I can do it."

Mr. Fitch's office was right by the front doors, which were unlocked.

They probably couldn't actually lock students in a building—fire codes and all that. She had Dom hold the door open, just in case it was locked from the outside, and stepped out into the night. It was perfectly clear and the moon was huge and full. The cold air raised goose bumps on her arms. Macy could smell smoke and she wondered if someone was already using a wood stove.

She picked up one of the jagged, decorative rocks from the front landscaping. Then she took off her shirt and wrapped it around the rock. Dom stared at her as she went back inside, lifted the rock, and shattered the window on the door. It was pretty loud. She had thought that wrapping the rock in her shirt might muffle the sound, but now there were little pieces of glass all over her shirt—she didn't think she should put it back on. Leaving her in just her bra and jeans. Great.

They stood perfectly still and posed to run for a full minute, but no one came.

"Here." Dom pulled off his shirt and handed it to her. "Give me yours." When she put on his shirt it was still warm and smelled like boy—some kind of aftershave or deodorant. Macy wanted to lift up the shirt and bury her face in it, but she also wanted to not look like a total creep.

Dom without a shirt was pretty amazing. Even in the dim light she could see the lines of his stomach and the top of his boxers where they peeked out from his jeans. She took a mental snapshot so she could give Claire details later. Macy briefly wondered what he would do if she reached out her hand and touched his chest where a few small hairs darkened his skin.

But Dom was shaking his head. "We should have just called Sam. She can actually pick locks."

Macy scowled. "It's open now, isn't it? Let's just take a look and get out of here." Dom wrapped Macy's shirt around his arm to protect himself from the broken glass, then reached in and unlocked the door. The inside of the room smelled just like she remembered—thick, sickeningly sweet incense. "Is that something from your ritual? That smell?"

"I don't know . . . I haven't actually seen one performed."

"Oh." Macy wrapped her arms around her chest. Dom's shirt hung down to the middle of her thighs. "I thought you were some kind of expert."

"Someone can be an expert without actually seeing something. What about the Big Bang? They don't actually have to see the beginning of the universe. Besides, I'm not really an expert."

"Okay, whatever. What are we looking for?"

"Something that belonged to the ghost."

"How will I know?"

"Just look for anything that seems out of the ordinary—not office supplies. It might be hair or bone. Tokens are often bone."

Macy had been rifling through the desk drawers, which were unlocked, when she pulled her hands back. Her stomach did a little somersault at the thought of touching a human bone. Dom was shining his flashlight around the room, looking in the trashcan and up on the walls. His beam rested on the picture of the old school.

"What's that?"

"The picture? It's the school before the Fire. From the 1920s or something."

Dom stepped closer to the photo. "I've seen this one before—we did some research before coming here. But I never noticed . . . ." He sucked in his breath. The light wobbled. "Macy. Come here."

Macy had just dumped out one of the drawers

and was sorting through thumbtacks, rubber bands, and sticky notes. She thought she found a condom, but it turned out to be an alcohol wipe. "What?"

"Come here," Dom said. "Now." His voice was a harsh whisper, which made her flinch.

She stopped what she was doing and went to him. He pointed up at the picture. The light reflected off the glass so it was hard to see at first what he was pointing to. But then she saw him: the man in coveralls wearing dark goggles over his eyes. He was in the background, behind the two boys. He wasn't in focus and Macy would never have noticed him had Dom not pointed it out. And even knowing he was in the picture, it was hard to look at him. It was like her eyes kept wanting to slide over him.

"Is that him?" Dom asked.

Macy nodded, then spun around, convinced that the ghost would be right behind her. She only managed to blind herself with Dom's flashlight. "Hell," she muttered, putting her hand to her eyes.

"Is that a picture of the ghost? Or do you think that's from when he was alive?"

"I have no idea. I've heard of ghosts showing up in old pictures, but those are usually fakes."

Macy studied the picture. It was too old, too grainy, to see if his clothes were covered in burns.

"Oh!" Macy turned to Dom. "Is that it? The link to the ghost—the Token?"

"An image of the ghost? I don't think so, but maybe we can find out who the ghost was from the picture."

"Maybe."

She looked back at the picture. Macy wondered how the man had died and why his ghost was still here. Why him? Why the woman in the theater? Why not Nick?

They rummaged around the office for a few more minutes. The drawers were mostly empty and they didn't find anything that looked important. Macy found a pack of gum and thought about slipping it into her pocket. She wondered how much trouble they could get into for breaking into Mr. Fitch's office. Would the police dust the drawers for fingerprints? Would they give her a dead-brother pass for this too?

"Do you hear that?" Dom asked. Macy paused, listening to the emptiness that sounded like static in her ears.

"I don't hear anything."

That's when she realized what was missing. The whole time they were in Mr. Fitch's office, they had heard the constant thump of distant music from the gym. Now the music was gone. Now they heard screaming.

Chapter Fourteen

They ran back toward the gym. If she had been watching the movie of her life, Macy would have told the girl who was barreling down the hall with a pack of gum still clenched in her fist to stop, run the other way. She would have told her to take out her phone and call 911. But this wasn't a movie, and all Macy could think about was that her friends were in there and they were screaming. Macy imagined Claire's shiny braids on fire, Jackson's face cracking as it burned. She kept running.

Smoke trickled out of the mostly-closed gym door. Macy clutched Dom's hand. She felt like she had swallowed something thick, like cough syrup.

"What do we do?" she whispered.

She waited for Dominick to take charge, to run inside or pull out his phone and call the cops. Instead, he lifted the hand holding Macy's and brought it close to his mouth. She thought for one surreal moment that he was going to kiss the back of her hand, like a character from a Jane Austen novel, but instead he raised a finger to his lips. "Shhh." They stood by the door, listening.

Now she could hear it. There were still screams, but also laughter. Someone ran past the door, shrieking and giggling, and it sounded like another person was fast on her heels. Macy let out her breath. The senior prank. Macy had completely forgotten about the senior fucking prank. She cracked the door open further and saw chaos.

Something that resembled the smoke you see at concerts drifted along the floor. Red lights moved through the room. People were running and shrieking and falling and laughing. Someone ran up to Macy and grabbed her arms. He cackled.

Even though Macy knew this must be the senior prank, she screamed bloody murder. Dom shined his flashlight and Macy saw that her assailant was wearing a ripped-up sheet with holes cut in the eyes. A ghost. The senior lifted his hand to Macy's face and wiped something wet onto her cheek. Then he ran away, whooping like a child playing cowboys and Indians.

Macy let out her breath. Her legs were actually quivering and the burn on her wrist pulsed with her heart. "Fucking seniors," she hissed. After a few minutes of dodging "ghosts," Macy and Dominick found the others standing in their corner of the gym, looking very annoyed. Dom lifted his flashlight: their faces were covered in what looked like blood.

"Are you okay?" Macy asked.

"Paint. Red fucking paint." Claire groaned. "I look like Carrie after the Prom. Right before she goes psycho and kills everyone." She held up a dripping red braid. "I don't even know if this is water soluble."

Trev had a red handprint in the middle of his face. "It got in my mouth," he said, and spit on the floor.

Macy put a hand to her own cheek—it came away red. "Bastards."

Claire pointed to one of the seniors running past. "I heard someone say that they were supposed to be the Ghosts of the Fire, or some shit like that, since I guess today is the anniversary. Pretty fucking insensitive after what happened yesterday, if you ask me. And they ruined my new pajamas." Claire sighed, holding her red hands out in front of her. "I'm going to the bathroom." Macy knew Claire was waiting for her to offer to go with her, but she didn't.

"Okay . . . Wish me luck."

Macy watched her friend shove her way through some "ghosts" on her way toward the girls' locker room.

Sam had red handprints on her chest and a swipe of red on her cheek. "So did you guys find something or what?" Then she looked Dom up and down. "Lose your shirt?"

"Something like that."

Dom had a stripe of red across his stomach, and a handprint on his butt. "We might have found something. A picture." He told them about the photograph in Mr. Fitch's office. "If we can find out who he was, that might help."

The running and shrieking was dying down and someone had turned the music back on. Macy could actually see a few ghosts rolling on the ground, making out in the red paint.

Trev took out his phone and began typing away with his thumbs. "This picture?" He showed it to Dom and Macy.

"Yeah, I think so," Dom said. "Can you figure out who's in it?"

After a few more minutes of typing, Trev

growled in frustration. "This town has a terrible web presence."

While Trev was looking at his phone, Macy realized that she hadn't seen Jackson since they returned to the gym. She looked around, trying to find his tall form among the other students. "Where's Jackson?"

Sam shrugged. "He got all pissy after you left with Dom. I think he wandered off somewhere."

Macy took out her phone and called Jackson. It rang and rang until it finally went to voicemail. "Wait, when was the last time you saw him?"

Trev was still looking at his phone, so Sam answered again. "Before the fuckwad seniors started their prank. He's probably in the bathroom or something."

Macy knew she should probably just let Jackson sulk by himself, but after all that screaming, she really wanted to see his face. She hesitated for a moment before ducking into the guys' locker room. The light—so bright compared to the dark of the gym—hurt her eyes. She had never been in a boy's bathroom before, let alone their locker room. There was a strange smell, like a sponge that had been left in the sink too long.

"Jackson?" she whispered. "Jackson, you here?"

Macy walked past the empty showers and toilets. Then she noticed that a door at the far end of the room leading out to the track was slightly ajar.

"Jackson?"

She walked past the windows to the coach's office toward the open door. Something moved in the corner of her eye—a shadow in the glass. Macy whipped her head around, peering in the window. No one was there except her own reflection.

It was so hot in the locker room. She lifted her hair off her neck, grimacing as the sweat on her back soaked into Dominick's shirt. Maybe Jackson had just stepped outside to get some air. She pressed her hand to the open door. The metal was warm to the touch. Macy could feel her heart beating right behind her eyes. She tried to swallow, but the spit stuck in her throat and she coughed.

Macy had always thought that she was brave. She killed spiders. She had never been afraid of the dark like Claire, who still kept a small nightlight in her room, though she would murder Macy if she ever told anyone. Macy had watched her first horror movie when she was just eight years old: *The Lost Boys*—that vampire movie with the actor from *24* before he got old. But in that moment, with her hand on the door, Macy didn't feel brave. She didn't want to be alone for another second. Turning around, Macy ran back toward the gym.

The locker room door swung shut behind her. It was so dark in the gym that Macy didn't see Trev until she had already collided with him. His phone spun out of his hands and cracked on the floor. "Ahh, shit! My phone!"

"Sorry!" Macy picked up the phone, wincing at the glowing, broken screen. "I'm really sorry. I just thought . . . "

"What happened?" Dom asked, taking the phone out of her hand and passing it back to Trev. She didn't get the chance to answer.

Chapter Fifteen

At first there was just a single shriek on the other side of the gym. The sound cut through the center of Macy's body and stole the air from her lungs. Macy gasped, then dug her fingernails into the palms of her hands. Were the seniors seriously doing this again? They had left the music on this time. It was a song Macy used to sing along to at middle school dances. Something slow.

Macy blinked, but it was so dark in the gym that she could barely tell the difference when her eyes were open or closed. Then a single orange light flamed on the far side of the gym, right by the main doors. There were more shrieks and a few nervous-sounding laughs.

Before Macy could even register what she was seeing, there was another light on the other side of the room next to the back doors. The orange lights flickered and seemed to grow taller as Macy stared. More people started to scream.

"What are they doing?" Macy breathed, taking a step backward, away from the lights. At her feet, a sleeping bag burst into flames, giving off the sour smell of burning plastic. Macy jumped aside, screaming.

Fanning the smoke from her eyes, Macy whipped her head left and right. Where was Dom? Claire? She couldn't see anyone. As she reached out in the smoky darkness, a hand reached back.

"Macy?"

It was Dom. He put a hand on her face, trying to see her by feel. "Are you hurt?"

"No," Macy answered, before doubling over

coughing. There was no air. "It's just the prank, right?"

Dom didn't answer. Maybe he couldn't hear her over all the screaming. She could barely hear her own voice. The lights were spreading up the walls and sprang up across the room like signal fires. No, the lights didn't just *look like* fire. They *were* fire.

Macy's stomach went cold and her teeth began to chatter. *Holy God.* The whole gym—everything—was burning. She pressed herself against Dom as though she could disappear inside him.

Then someone ran past, covered in flames. As the student brushed against Macy and Dom, the tips of Macy's hair curled from the heat. She screamed again, dancing away from the burning kid. Macy closed her eyes and covered her ears.

Dom forced her hands down from the sides of her face. "Go!" he yelled into her ear. "Outside!"

Macy made herself open her eyes. It was one of the hardest things she'd ever done. At first, all she could see was a red haze. Then the scene before her took shape. Huge, orange flames dripped down the walls, licking across the bleachers. Looking up, the ceiling was a swirling mass of fire. Macy flinched when the glass of a nearby basketball hoop shattered and a new wave of screams swallowed the tinkling of the falling glass.

She could just barely see what appeared to be crowds of kids gathered around the exits, but it didn't look like anyone was getting out. They were just writhing in the flickering light, pushing each other. A few people rolled on the ground, covered in flames. She could smell them, she realized suddenly, could smell their flesh burning. The screaming had finally drowned out the music. Or else the speakers were on fire too.

Macy turned back toward the locker room. She tried to open the door, but immediately drew her hand back. The handle was too hot to touch. Macy pressed it anyway, covering her hand with Dom's long shirt. It was locked.

"It won't open!" Macy screamed. Then Dom's

hands were on her shoulders, wrenching her away from the door. Fire now covering the locker room door like a bright silk curtain where she had just been standing. The heat felt like a hand smothering her face. She couldn't breathe.

"It has to be the ghost! He locked the fucking doors!" Dom yelled as he pulled Macy away from the burning wall, toward the center of the gym. "Trev? Sam? You there?"

"The bag's on fire." Sam's voice was just behind them. "But we got 'em."

"Do what you can!" Then Dom pulled Macy close so his cheek was touching hers. Both their faces were slick with sweat. "Macy, I need your help. You need to look. Help me find the ghost. We can still stop this!"

Trembling, Macy once again forced herself to look around the gym. At first, all she could see was fire, smoke, the twisting shadows of burning students. How could she find one ghost in Hell?

Then, she saw him. Macy had been looking for

a ghost made of fire, but what she finally noticed was the absence of it. He was standing about fifteen feet directly in front of her, leaning against the wall. The fire curved around him, but did not touch him—a dark void among the flames.

As Macy tried to make out the ghost's features through the smoke, her shoes caught fire. She kicked them off, shrieking, wrenching herself away from Dom. Then she heard a loud "whooshing" sound and her feet were covered in white foam.

Fire extinguishers. Trev and Sam had brought fire extinguishers. She fucking loved Trev and Sam. Looking wildly around her, Macy saw that the twins were spraying everything—even students who weren't already on fire.

"I see him!" Macy yelled, pointing toward the dark shape. "The ghost—he's right there."

"Where? I can't see him." Dom took a step in the direction Macy pointed, shielding his face from the heat. "He's not there," he said. "Oh shit!" Then he swung around toward her, gripping her shoulders. "I didn't think of it before, but I never saw him. I never fucking saw the ghost, did I? I can't see him."

"What?"

"I can't see him. I don't think I could ever see him. But you can! You have to fight him!"

Macy shrugged off Dom's hands. "I can't! I don't know how." She took a step back, but stopped. There was nowhere to go that wasn't burning. Nowhere except the ghost.

Dominick coughed, fanning the smoke away from his face. "You can. Because if you don't do this, then you'll die. And I'll die. And everyone in this fucking room will die."

"What do I do?" Macy stared at the ghost. She could just barely make out his face. He was smiling, but in the red, smoky glow it looked like a grimace.

"Close your eyes. Picture the ghost dissolving. Imagine every piece of him drifting away like smoke on the wind."

Macy closed her eyes and pictured the ghost.

First, she imagined him ripped apart—arms and legs flying in different directions. Then, she dissolved his body in a vat of acid, letting him melt until even his goggles were pools of black ink on the surface.

She opened her eyes and he was still there.

She imagined a wolf chewing on his body, tearing out his intestines like a red ribbon unspooling.

Macy opened her eyes again. The ghost was still staring at her. Still smiling.

"It's not working!"

"Just concentrate!" Dom yelled back. "You just need to concentrate!"

All around her people were screaming. The fire was so hot that the hair on her arms was smoking. Macy's stomach was a seething furnace and her hands shook as she started walking, closing the distance between her and the ghost.

Ten feet.

"Coward!" she screamed at him.

Five feet.

"You like killing kids? Fucking coward!"

She didn't stop until she was close enough to touch the ghost. She could have reached out and pulled off his goggles. Instead, she grabbed the blowtorch from his hands. It was solid, and so hot that she almost dropped it. Even through the deafening screams, Macy could hear her skin sizzling.

"Let me go." The ghost's voice was a whisper, but it sounded like it was directly inside her head. For an instant, it was all she could hear.

Screaming, Macy lifted the blowtorch and brought it down on the side of ghost's head. There was a sickening crunch and something that looked like oil oozed down his face. The ghost brought his empty hands to his head, still smiling. She hit him again and again—her arms aching with the shock of each blow. He fell to his knees, looking up at her through the blank, empty gaze of his goggles.

"Not enough," he whispered as he disappeared.

The blowtorch vanished from her blistered

hands. Then the room, which had been lit up with the shaky, reddish light of the fires, was plunged back into darkness.

The fires, she realized, were out.

Chapter Sixteen

Macy took a deep breath—in through her nose, out through her mouth—then starting coughing so hard her lungs felt like they were burning too. Dominick caught her elbow, keeping her upright. "Is he gone?"

She nodded. "But he said something. He said, 'not enough.'"

"Oh my God," Dom breathed. "I forgot about Mr. Fitch. The ghost will just come back if we don't find Mr. Fitch and destroy the Token."

"But where would he be?" Macy's ears felt like they were stuffed with cotton. The screaming had stopped and in its place were whispers and moans and quiet, muffled sobbing. Then it started to rain. Macy stopped and looked up into the blackness, water dripping down her face. It couldn't rain inside. A wave of relief washed through her. She must be dreaming.

Macy almost laughed out loud, but then she heard Trev say, "About fucking time the sprinklers turned on." For a moment Macy thought she was going to throw up, but she managed to bite back the rising bile. She clenched her fists over her stomach and took a step closer to Dom.

Dominick had his flashlight out again and shined the light around the gym. The air was so full of smoke and falling water that it was hard to see anything. It looked like someone had opened the main doors. People were leaving. Macy saw a few motionless, smoking piles and she hoped they weren't students, but what else could they be?

"He's probably outside," Dom finally said. "I bet he kept a safe distance while he tried to burn us alive." His voice was low and raspy, tinged with something dangerous. Macy didn't think she'd ever heard him truly angry before. She hoped he'd tear Mr. Fitch's throat out with his teeth.

Dom rounded up Sam and Trev, who had abandoned their empty fire extinguishers, and the four of them headed for the boys locker room. The door was no longer locked, and swung open as soon as Sam pressed on the handle. Macy led them to the propped open door and Dom nodded, putting his finger to his lips. She knew that Dom expected to find Mr. Fitch right outside the gym with something that could control the ghost: this Token. Whatever the fuck that was.

The fresh night air made Macy weep with relief. She wiped the tears from her face and her hands came away sticky—paint or smoke residue. Macy pushed her wet hair off her forehead.

"Where is he?" she whispered. They looked all around. In the distance, Macy could hear the swell of sirens. She wondered where all of the chaperones were: if the ghost had burned them too, or if they had called 911 when they heard screaming and couldn't open the gym doors. Macy realized that she still didn't know where Claire was, or Jackson, but she had no time to think about them. Macy saw someone across the track, standing next to the far fence.

As the four of them jogged toward the figure, Macy had no idea how they were going to deal with Mr. Fitch. He was so tall. His shadow stretched out far behind him, cast by the nearly full moon. But when they got closer, Macy saw that it wasn't Mr. Fitch standing by the fence.

It was Jackson.

"Motherfucker!" Dominick whispered.

It didn't look like Jackson had seen them yet. He was facing out, toward the wreckage of the old school across the fence.

"Jackson!" Macy called before Sam put a hand over her mouth.

"Shhh!" Sam hissed.

Macy wrenched herself away from Sam.

"Don't touch me! Don't fucking touch me! Jackson!"

She ran to her friend, sprinting in her bare feet across the damp grass with Sam and the others just a step behind her.

Macy stopped a few feet from Jackson and hugged herself with her aching arms. "Jackson? Are you okay?"

He turned. There were tears on his face.

"I'm sorry," he whispered.

In the distance she could hear the sirens getting louder. Macy hugged herself tighter, taking a step back just as Dominick caught up.

"You? You did this?" Dom yelled, and would probably have thrown himself at Jackson, but Macy held him back—her feet skidding on grass and her hands burning. In the shadows, just across the fence, was another person. A short, thin woman, wearing a white dress that looked like a nightgown. She was holding a gun.

"Lorna?" Macy said. Her first thought was that the old woman had somehow wandered out of Western Winds and gotten lost. Macy was just wondering if she should call 911, like a million police weren't already on the way, or if she should just walk her the two blocks back to the retirement home, when she noticed the bracelet. Lorna's charm bracelet—strung with so many tiny bones—dangled from her raised arm. *Bones*. That must be the Token!

"Oh my God," Macy said. It was Lorna. All along it had been Lorna—not Mr. Fitch—who had been controlling the ghost. Macy's hands curled at her sides. She wanted to claw the old woman's face.

"I'm sorry." Jackson said again—his voice thick with tears. "I went outside to look around and I found her out here. She wouldn't let me go. I should have tried—I could hear screaming."

Lorna watched Macy, all the while keeping the gun level with Jackson's heart. Through the wire fence, her face looked like it had been stitched together.

"You ruined it," Lorna finally said in a low voice. "Did you know I've waited fifty years for this? Fifty years? Well, it can still work. You—all of you," she gestured with her gun. "Come with me."

There was a hole in the fence. Someone— probably Lorna—had snipped it clean with wire cutters. Lorna made Jackson go first, then the twins. Sam's hair caught on the fence, and Macy's heart twitched when Sam ripped it free, leaving behind a thick clump of hair. Lorna kept the gun pointed at Macy's head while she ducked through.

"Keep those hands up," Lorna directed. "And start walking, single file."

Macy raised her hands higher, then asked, "Where are we going?"

Lorna laughed—a strange, soft laugh. "Isn't that

what we all want to know? Where are we going? You're going to find out. Just a few more minutes."

Lorna made them stop when they reached a small clearing in the woods. Among the shadows of the trees, Macy could see the metal frame of an old swing set that was overgrown with blackberry vines. All around the clearing were piles of bricks and other remnants of the old school.

"What are we doing here?" Dom asked. He was standing to Macy's left and Jackson and the twins were on her right. Lorna stood in front of them, sometimes pointing the gun at Macy, sometimes at Trev or Sam.

"We're waiting," the old woman said, "for the Door to open."

"But we stopped you," Trev said, his voice a rough whisper. "We stopped your fucking ritual." Out of the corner of her eye, Macy saw Sam take a step closer to her brother and thread her fingers through his.

Lorna shook her head. "You think I *want* this Door to open? Idiots."

While still aiming the gun at them, Lorna touched the bracelet with her other hand. "Come," she called out. "Come here now."

The air in front of Lorna started to waver and the ghost appeared. He was whole, with no trace of the damage Macy had inflicted on him. The ghost faced them and seemed to look right at Macy. He touched his wrist, echoing Lorna's motion. "Now," he whispered, and again, it felt like his words were inside Macy's head. "Do it now."

Macy didn't think. She lunged, pushing Lorna's gun away with one hand and grabbing the bracelet with the other—ripping it off Lorna's wrist. The ghost vanished. As the carved bones scattered into the night, the gun fired. Dominick fell back with a cry, clutching his shoulder.

Lorna gave a raw, earsplitting scream that scraped along Macy's spine. The old woman dropped the gun and put her hands to her chest as though she was the one who had been shot. She screamed again, raising her face to the sky. Macy had never heard a sound like it. It was worse than Mr. Bishop's scream as he'd burned in the classroom. Worse even than the students in the gym. The only thing she could compare it to was the time her mother backed over a neighbor's cat and it let out a horrific yowl as it died. That was what Lorna sounded like—a dying animal. For a brief moment, Macy wondered if Nick had screamed like that when his car crashed.

"You should have let me," Lorna moaned. "Just let me do it. You don't know what you've done!" She howled again, sinking to her knees.

"You killed people!" Macy screamed down at her. "They were burning!"

Lorna turned an accusing gaze to Macy. The moonlight smoothed the wrinkles from her face, and the tears made her cheeks shine like polished stone. Macy couldn't even see her scars.

"You've unleashed hell upon us," Lorna

screamed, taking a deep, gasping breath. "The fire would have kept the Door closed, just like it did fifty years ago. But you've ruined it." Lorna bent down. She seemed to be trying to find the lost pieces of bone in the dirt and leaves. Macy almost reached out her hand toward the woman. She was still furious, but Lorna, weeping, crawling on her hands and knees on the cold ground, was a pitiful thing.

Then Macy jerked her hand away and stepped back, letting Jackson's arms enfold her from behind. He put his head on top of hers and she sank back into him, her teeth chattering. As thoughts spun through Macy's head—call the police, get help for Dom, try to explain that this old lady is a murderer—Lorna looked up.

Her face twisted.

"No!" Lorna cried, holding out her empty hands. Right in front of her was the ghost. He held his own hands out, then placed them on Lorna's arms. Macy could hear flesh burning. Then the ghost wrapped his arms around the old woman. It could have been a hug, except that Lorna was screaming. A thin banner of smoke rose above them and Macy could smell Lorna's hair, her dress, burning.

The air crackled and singed hair stood up on Macy's arms.

"What's happening?" Jackson whispered into her hair.

"I don't know," she said. Her mouth tasted like blood. Macy saw Sam and Trev kneeling beside Dominick, who lay motionless on the ground. The crackling grew louder. Trees shook, and the twisted metal of the old burned playground groaned. Macy's ears hurt, like the time she flew in a plane with a bad cold and her ears wouldn't pop and the pressure made them feel like they were going to bleed. Jackson held her tighter.

Then the night exploded.

A great light radiated out from where the ghost was holding Lorna in his fiery embrace. Macy was thrown back, landing on top of Jackson. She couldn't see anything. Even when she opened her eyes as wide as they would go, everything was the same blinding white. Macy sank her fingers into the dirt, her burned hands almost beyond pain. The light shrank until she could see fallen leaves by her face and Dominick on his side—his chest rising and falling as blood ran down his arm.

Lorna and the ghost were gone, and in their place was a rippling sheet of light. Macy raised her blistered hand to the light.

"Nick?" she whispered, tears leaking out of the corners of her eyes. "Are you there?"